PRAISE FOR SEAN GATES AND
THE FIRST HARRY COGBILL MYSTERY

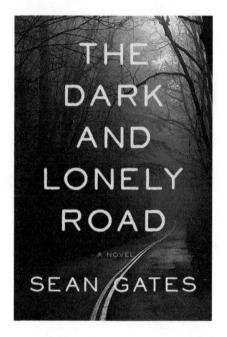

"The Dark and Lonely Road by Sean Gates takes us on a thrilling journey of re-demption, love, and second chance...beautifully written...a scintillating read." - - **OnlineBookClub**

"...Readers will be attracted to this Southern tale of a broken man with some-thing to prove and a reason for proving it." **-- Kirkus Reviews**

To
MARTHA V.
LET YOUR
SPIRIT BE A
LIGHT...

IN THE
TRACKLESS
WILD

A HARRY COGBILL NOVEL

IN THE TRACKLESS WILD

A HARRY COGBILL NOVEL

SEAN GATES

First Printing: 2024

ISBN 978-1-304-03714-5

Used Books
PO Box 352 Dahlgren, VA, 22448

For Gene;
Harry's friend and mine

And whenever I remember, sirs,
The country of my birth
I feel that I am just as good
As any man on earth;
And I proudly doff my hat, sirs,
And make a bow profound
To the land that's standing still, sirs,
While the vulgar world goes round.

—*From* Old King George, A Saga of the Happy Horse and Buggy Days, *by Thomas Lomax Hunter*

ACKNOWLEDGEMENTS

WRITING is a solitary process but no book is possible without the help of others. For this book I am indebted as ever to the people of King George County, the finest bunch of yahoos on the planet. In particular I need to thank friends both old and new: Mrs. Ellen Clare Washington, who reached out to me with stories about her father, L.V. Clare, and the rest of her family, and in so doing taught me about some local figures and iconic local businesses past that I knew only in name. Mrs. Anne Guilliams of Spotsylvania County, who likewise reached out with stories of her own, involving an old King George mystery that strangely echoed aspects of the plot from "Dark and Lonely," and helped draw into focus the darker side of King George in 1959-60.

Once again Elizabeth Nuckols Lee and Jean Moore Graham's "King George County, A Pictorial History" has been an invaluable asset, as has the wonderful Lewis Egerton Smoot Memorial Library and its excellent staff. Likewise I owe thanks to Junior and Marcy Morris, Hal Revercomb, Matt Clift, and Jason Morgan, who filled in some blanks in my knowledge of local history. Any errors are entirely my own. Tina Twigg-James and Pat Raynor, for pointing me in the right direction. Erin Scroggs, for driving me out to Nanzatico, giving me a tour of the area, and a well-timed push when my creative engine had stalled.

To all my extended family at Trinity United Methodist Church, my friends at Food Lion #1582, and my friends throughout the community who encourage me in a million ways every day. And to Adil "AJ" Jeddou, Herman MacDonald, and Beverly Lanham at Pizza Bono, for great service and keeping me well-fed. My friends and colleagues in the Rappatomac Writers Group for feedback on these chapters and motivating me to keep working when I was adrift at the midpoint – in Particular Stan Parsons, Denise DeVries, and Nan Harvey. Kris Williams, whose friendship and encouragement are always a light in dreary weather.

A big thank you to my friend Shari Miller for her love and support, who along with Clayton Spinney and my parents Rob and Beverly Gates, read this stuff when I'm not sure if I've made chicken salad or something a little less appetizing. Speaking of love and support, as always I owe thanks to my colleagues Neil Richard, Sarah Snow, and Jeremy Bertz at Project94, to my sister Sinay Ou, and my brother Darek McGee, who has been my companion in exploring the mysteries of King George County since about 1979. Thanks again to Lina: without your encouragement I wouldn't have published "The Dark and Lonely Road," and it is doubtful this book would exist.

And of course to each of you, my readers: stories are, after all, for sharing.

CHAPTER ONE

"HEY. HEY Hare, you got a minute?"

The bus boy was a little Italian guy with one leg about three inches shorter than the other. He stood about 5'4" and had his hair – what there was of it – buzzed down in something like a high-and-tight. He was olive-complected and there were always dark circles under his eyes. He gimped around with a tub full of dirty dishes on his hip looking like he might collapse at any minute, but I never heard him complain about the work. To be fair, he'd have been hard-pressed to fit any complaints in among all the questions he never stopped asking.

"I've got about a second, Joey. What is it?"

A tall black man in a greasy apron brought me a couple of burger patties from the prep cooler and I tossed them on the flat top beside a couple slices of rye bread, a trio of hot dogs, a pair of sunnyside eggs and a furiously sizzling heap of corned beef hash. Plates and forks were clanging behind me and Joey was in everybody's way.

"You wan'me put these dirty dishes back by the sink?"

"On the cart, Joey, same as I told you ten minutes ago."

For more than a year, I'd been a grill cook at Horne's in Port Royal across the Rappahannock from my King George home.

Horne's was an east coast chain of combination restaurant/gift shops designed to compete with Stuckey's and Howard Johnson's. The trademark was a steeply pitched yellow roof. I scanned the tickets clipped to the hood above me, making sure I hadn't forgotten anything. A waitress' face appeared in the serving window.

"Where's that corned beef hash?"

"I don't know but I got a sausage for you," the head cook hollered back.

"Fucksakes, Murray."

"It's a kitchen, Harry," Murray growled. "Grow a pair."

"A-and the forks and spoons and whatnot go in the basket, right?"

"Yes Joey, in the basket!"

"Okay, okay, I got this."

I grabbed a clean plate, scooped the eggs and the hash onto it, and slid it on the counter under the warming lamps.

Joey still stood there grinning like a moron.

"I tell ya, we're gonna get us some beers and a bushel a crabs one of these nights, Hare."

"And don't call me Hair, all I can picture is the floor of a barbershop."

"Yer more like a bunnyrabbit, Cogbill."

Joey's New York accent was a neon sign hanging over his head, and the burning letters spelled "COME-HERE." Perhaps I should explain. To many locals, people were divided into two groups, "from-heres" and "come-heres," and nothing about Joey left you any room for doubt. Most of the others wouldn't

have much to do with him. I didn't blame them, exactly; he was annoying as hell and despite his claim of ten years' restaurant experience he was a month in and needed his hand held for every single task. We were never getting that bushel of crabs. Hell, I didn't like crabs any better than I liked Joey.

It turned out neither of us would even finish our shifts. Half an hour and the same conversation twice again later, Joey came slipping in through the swinging door, dumped his tub of dirty dishes and himself all over the red-clay tile floor, and staggered, greasy and only slightly bleeding, to his uneven feet.

"I gotta get outta here, Harry. Holy Jesus, I gotta go."

He yanked loose his apron strings as he hurried away and nearly decapitated himself when the apron snagged on a wire rack full of supplies. He wrestled with it comically for a moment, then got his head free and scurried away, leaving the apron where it hung entangled with the rack.

I don't know why I went after him, pity or sympathy or simple-minded kindness. I guess I had never quite felt I fit in anywhere, and no matter how much Joey got under my skin, I didn't have it in me to treat him unkindly.

I caught up to him fumbling with the keys to the deep-sea green '53 Bel Air that sat hunched behind the cinderblock building like a frightened scarab, the sun glaring off the windshield.

"What happened, Joey?"

He dropped the keys and jumped so high I thought he could have cleared the hood of the car.

"Jesus you scared the shit outta me. I can't talk now, Cogbill. I got to go."

"You know you're liable to get fired for just abandoning your post like that."

He'd recovered his keys and clambered into his car.

"You think I don't know that? Fuck man, this is my life we're talking about here. I got a wife and a kid. Sorry 'bout them crabs, we woulda had some fun. It was nice knowin' ya, man. You always been straight wit' me."

"Joey what the hell?"

But the motor sputtered to life and the car beetled backward, the wheels squeaking and something rattling like a tin can full of stones. Then the green insectoid shape farted a dark cloud of exhaust and rattled out onto 17, roaring across 301 and west towards New Post.

"Cogbill, breaktime's over -- we got about a dozen orders up and my grill cook's out here jawing with the single worst busboy I ever had the misfortune of knowing."

"I'm on it, Murray."

But I couldn't help wondering what had gotten into Joey. He was as scared as any human being I'd ever seen, and I had been in Ardennes during what the press insisted on calling the Battle of the Bulge; an altogether too frivolous name for Hell on Earth.

Instead of going straight back to the flat-top grill where I toiled ten hours a day, I made my way through the kitchen and out to the area behind the soda counter with the striped awning called the Circus Grille, where a milkshake machine whirred and soda fountains pissed Coca-Cola into frosted glasses heaped with ice.

Kids were spinning on intentionally mismatched vinyl stools lining the counter, a group of Army guys from AP Hill were trooping in through the gift shop, the L-shaped row of booths populated by singles and couples traveling north or south on 301, Florida to New York, New York to Florida, and everyplace in between. Most of them weren't locals, so there was nothing really to see; men in blazers and sport shirts, women in sporty dresses or capris and blouses, their hair covered in scarves or held up with sunglasses. This time of year, which way they were going was usually indicated by how deeply they were or were not tanned. There was nothing here that would have stood out on any given day.

"Excuse me," said a voice to my left, and I turned to see a well-dressed man about my age, tall and broad-shouldered, his hair lacquered down and his smile flawless and broad. He wore a couple of rings, a gold watch, and a thin gold chain around his neck, which was just visible at his throat where the collar of his sport-shirt was laid open. His blazer was tailored and apart from a scar that cut his left eyebrow, he was immaculate. Black hair, olive complection, strong nose, dimpled chin.

"Yes?"

"I believe your busboy may have stolen my wallet." The accent was New York, probably Brooklyn but I'd only lived there for a short while and my ear wasn't the most refined.

"Which one?"

"Short guy, a dago like me. Bum leg."

The casual way he said dago matched the scar above his eye; small imperfections in his otherwise flawless mask.

"He just took off," I said. "We'll call the police."

"That's a joke, right? Sheriff Taylor and Deputy Fife are going to recover my wallet?"

"I could at least take your name," I said. "In case someone finds it?"

I grabbed for a ticket pad that was resting on the counter, and slid it towards him. His hand went absently to his jacket pocket for his own pen, and came out with a wallet.

"Well, would you look at that? I thought it was in my pants. My apologies to Tony."

"Joey," I said.

"Of course. I was thinking of someone I know. I guess your Tony reminds me of him."

"Joey," I said again.

"Joey, right. Slip of the tongue."

"Cogbill what the hell are you doing?"

"Relax, Murray, I'm helping a customer."

"That ain't your job, Cogbill. You belong behind the scenes. Making food. That's what we do here, remember?"

"Not now, Murray."

"That's right, I forgot you sign my checks," Murray said. "Oh. Wait. You don't. Get back to work."

I came out from behind the counter and pushed back through the swinging door into the kitchen, but I could feel my hands shaking and my nerves were jangling like piano strings.

"I need that hot roast beef," the waitress said at the window.

"I thought you'd never ask," Murray hollered back.

I'm not entirely clear on what happened next; there was a sound like rending fabric behind my eyes and drums pounding in my ears, and the next thing I knew I was standing over Murray; he was sprawled on the kitchen floor with all the color drained out of his face, blood running out of a gash on his forehead, and my apron stuffed in his mouth. Strong black arms were wrapped around my chest pulling me back.

"It ain't worth it, Mr. Harry."

"William. What happened?"

"You done busted up Mr. Murray."

"I guess I'm fired."

"Yeah I bet you is."

Murray just gawked up at me, unspeaking, and I realized he'd urinated on himself.

"It was a lousy job anyway," I said.

"Well hey there, you're home early."

Ethel Burkitt had come in from the garden, and stood in our kitchen sort of hipshot in her shapeless overalls and too-big flannel shirt, the sleeves rolled midway up her forearms. Dust from the yellow earth covered her knees and backside. It was late September, and the trees were kissed by the first spark of autumn. As it always did from May to October, the sun had turned her light brown hair to copper-gold, and raised a dusting of freckles across her cheeks and nose. She had a basket of squash and zucchini nestled on her hip, and her eyes were the color of cobalt as she looked up at me, twisting her mouth to one side as far as it would go.

"Surprise," I said.

"Is ever'thin' okay?"

I reflexively ran a hand across the back of my neck, unable to meet her eyes.

She put the basket down on the counter, and studied me. I could not hide the shame I felt. I could never hide anything from her. She saw right through me, and had from the moment she arrived at my door. It was one of the reasons I loved her; the hand that wrought our souls had joined them long before the day her red pickup had rattled up my drive in a cloud of ochre dust.

"I don't deserve you."

"Don't stand there expecting me to absolve you of anything, 'cos I cain't."

I didn't quite know what to say.

"I don't know what's wrong with me. I thought...I don't know."

"And don't start with that, either. I cain't deal with it right now."

She shucked off the overalls, her sturdy legs pale beneath the hem of the flannel shirt as she started for the hall. She wheeled to face me again, and I braced myself.

"Do you know why you cain't hold down a job, Hiermus?"

"Oh here we go."

"It's because all these damn jobs is beneath you."

I wasn't sure much of anything was beneath me. I'd let my best friend take a grenade for me in Ardennes, gotten kicked out of the Army, and fired from about everything else in the last twenty-plus years. When I met Ethel she'd asked me to help her with some bad guys causing trouble for her family, but she wound up saving herself. Which explained why I married her, but not so much why she'd married me.

"If you understood half of what you--no, forget it. I need a shower."

Outside the sky grew swiftly dark and the trees across the fields began to sway, the grasses and wildflowers rippling like the surface of the sea. Our rescue fox, Fawkes, came charging in through his doggie-door and scurried under the bed. The sky strobed with electricity as a sound like sustained ordnance rolled across the countryside, and with a roar what seemed like an entire ocean blasted across our fields and tattooed the tin roof of our house.

I started to follow her, then thought better of it. At that moment I couldn't imagine why I'd ever believed I could have a happy life like other people. Ethel was seventeen years my junior, confident, assertive, witty; everything I was not. I could not conceive of a universe in which I deserved her love, but neither could I imagine my life without her. The only thing that really wounded me was knowing I had let her down.

That notion was reinforced when she opened the bathroom door post-shower wrapped in a robe to dry her hair, as though we had never bathed or lain together, and would not look at me. These small acts of withholding intimacy pierced me like tiny daggers. I felt foolish, embarrassed by the lies my heart had perpetrated against me.

CHAPTER TWO

I SPENT most of the next day feeling sorry for myself, and Ethel spent it mainly avoiding me. She left in the morning without saying anything, but her clothes were still in the closet and I assumed she hadn't left me. Even Fawkes seemed to avoid me. I made a pot of coffee, fried three eggs and far too much bacon, then ate it all.

Even these smells did not draw the little fuzzbutt from his pen. I put on my coat and hat and went for a walk around the property, counted butterflies among the thistle and a cardinal somewhere in the big yellow poplar singing birdy-birdy-birdy at the top of his tiny lungs.

But neither these beauties nor the sunlight that saturated them could lift my spirits. I needed to be proactive, but first I needed to grieve the loss of my job and the loss of normalcy in my marriage. I had to remind myself of what I had been before Ethel came along. That's a lie: I was wallowing, punishing myself for being myself. I did not deserve happiness and rather than simply pick it up where it lay, I would throw it far from my person and accept my sad fate. What would Ethel say if she were around? She'd tell me to stop beating myself up and go be the man she knew me to be.

But she wasn't around.

Frank Burkitt rose in the morning with the empty space on Alice's side of the bed as it had been for years, and the solitude in the gloom of the upstairs hallway, the cruel desolation of Ethel's abandoned bedroom. Pale blue light emanated through the drawn curtains and settled around the shoe molding, the grey clouds of his mood like cobwebs in the corners of the ceiling.

A stranger sneered at him from the bathroom mirror, with haunted eyes of volcanic glass ringed in folds of purple, his sunken jaws frosted with silver like the cattle gate at dawn in February. Even his clothing seemed to belong to another man: his undershirt draped like a slackened sail across the knobs of his shoulders, his arms corded and twisted like wild vines, and his trousers, seldom washed, hung from his suspenders for they scarce would touch the desiccated saddle of his hips.

He made coffee. Once he had taken it with cream and sugar, but nothing much pleased him anymore and it did not seem worth the bother, so he drank it black and bitter and felt no particular disgust. He burned his eggs and bacon, and could not get his toast to brown. Indeed it emerged from the toaster white and soft regardless of the setting, until on the second pass it invariably returned black and crumbling with ash. He nibbled at the pitiful breakfast, and threw most of it to the pigs as he did every day.

He fed his animals but rarely found hours enough in the day to tend to the other chores. He told himself that he was old, and tired; and though this could not fairly be disputed, neither was it the reason he seldom rose before ten and rarely embarked upon labor of any kind before he'd pushed a late lunch around his plate and sent it after the breakfast.

When Ethel's red F-1 clattered up the driveway to her childhood home, she found her father deep into his morning jug. She climbed down off the running board beneath a gunmetal sky, and squinted at her father where he sat slouched on the porch.

Creeper had heaved through the planks and snarled around the posts.

"Franklin Burkitt, what are you doing?"

"Still your daddy, either if you live here or not."

"Then goddamned act like it. I swear y'all are all alike."

"You come out here just to scold me, or you want to burn the house down? Ain't much left in this old pot but I reckon it'll do."

"I was wondering if you were going to give us a pig like we discussed. I'll pay you for it but right now I'm gonna have to owe you."

"Ain't been to the butcher. Have to pick one out and take him yourself."

"It don't look like you done much but drink yourself stupid. Find yourself a wife, daddy, or hire some help. Or get some help."

Frank grunted.

"Daddy Franklin, I love you and I am worried."

"Taking that pig or what?"

She stormed off toward the barn.

"Take the big one. Can't feed him no more."

She returned a few moments later and loaded a good-sized shoat into the back of the truck.

"You're better than this."

"You know how I feel about that man, and you married him anyway, so don't come here and tell me what I am or what I ought to be."

"Did you think I was gonna stay here forever and be a spinster? Daddy's little girl when I'm old and grey?"

"I'll just go the hell on and die, then."

She marched up and knocked the jug out of his hand, and he slapped her.

She stared at him with wide eyes, and he looked up at her from his seat, his lip quivering, and the corners of his eyes began to glisten.

"Momma would be ashamed of you."

"I'm sorry, pumpkin. I'm so sorry."

"You know what the best apology is, daddy? Changed behavior. I grew up and got married. It's what people do. And I sure to God have enough problems not dealing with your bullshit. I cain't fix you or him or anyone else, but I'll be damned if I let you sit here and drink yourself to death while everything you built crumbles around you. Now you're welcome at the barbecue, but for God's sake, take a shower and shave, and leave the jug at home."

When I got back from my walk I made more coffee and started thinking about lunch. I made a couple of sandwiches, tossed a salad and waited for Ethel. When she did return, we both just picked at our food.

"Did you apply for many jobs?"

"No."

"What did you do?"

"Nothing much."

"Well for God's sake Hieronymus, they don't come door-to-door."

I spent most of the next day working in the backyard. We'd lately planned a barbecue, by which I mean to say that Ethel had planned a barbecue and I had humored her because I wanted her to be happy. Although I was glad to smoke a pig and make up a batch of my sauce and a bowl of slaw, I'd have preferred the two of us ate it rather than hosting a party, but I was old enough and wise enough to know it wasn't all about me. So, hoping to win back Ethel's favor, I set about digging a square pit. I could see Ethel in the garden, but she did not speak to me nor I to her, for fear I would only be reminded of her disappointment and I did not feel I had much farther to fall.

By evening I had finished the pit, lined it with cinderblocks along the sides, and filled the bottom with gravel. Ethel had long-since retired to the house. In the lengthening shadows I thought I saw a figure at the edge of the forest, far across the lawn and the fields of wildflowers split with fences draped in vine.

I dragged an arm across my bleary eyes and looked again, and the figure was gone. In my darkest moments it was not un-usual that I would be visited by the shade of Rollie Taylor, my Army buddy who'd saved my life when he threw himself on a grenade in Ardennes. I was never sure if he was real or just my way of reminding myself of the inevitability of my failure.

On the third day I rose from the dead, drove into King George Courthouse, parked my car at Trinity Methodist and walked over to the Courthouse Market. Morris wasn't hiring, but he indicated he'd keep me in mind. I walked the narrow sidewalk on that side of Route 3, tried Morris Chevrolet and then passed the old bank building across the street from Trinity. There were four or five little homes in bungalow fashion, loft windows facing the sidewalk above covered porches, the painted brick exterior and bright red door of St. John's Episcopal across the street. Little Hudson cemetery on a rise overlooking the road.

There were some older houses, a tin-roofed affair with a wide gallery porch much like my own. Indiantown Road went off to the right, Clift's garage on the left, and the little fire station was across the street, next to the Clift Ford dealership. There was nothing further on my side of the road, except to follow the narrow sidewalk past Pinehurst and around the bend at St. Anthony's of Padua onto the loop of old Route 3 that went past the schools.

There was no reason to go that way, nothing there but the two schools side by side, so I crossed 3 and tried Clift's Ford. Not being a mechanic or a natural salesman, I didn't get far but I'd have welcomed a change. Maybe I'd try Conor Clare's Pontiac dealership up the road.

Instead I sucked it up and went next door to Tommy's Snack Bar, adjoined to the large Ford dealership. It was named for Earl Thomas Clift Jr., paralyzed in a car accident. I guess on paper it was his but mostly his mother, Ruth Clare Clift, ran it. There were a few booths down both walls with teal benches and formica tops, a few tables in the middle, and a counter with stools across the back separating the kitchen from the little dining room.

"I'm staffed mister, sorry."

"Guess I'll settle for a sandwich and a cup of coffee?"

"That I can do."

I sat on one of the stools. There was a hat shop upstairs, but I didn't figure it took more than one fellow to sell hats, so I decided to skip it. I sent the cream and sugar back and sat there drinking my coffee, flipping through a *Free Lance-Star* someone had left on the counter.

As I thumbed through the classifieds I had to reflect on some of my recent decisions. I shouldn't have hit Murray. I shouldn't have involved myself in Joey's business or spoken to the man with the scarred eyebrow. I shouldn't have dragged Ethel into the pit that was my life.

But this line of thought wasn't useful; given time and enough self-pity I could trace it clear back through Ardennes at least as far as my birth in Chesterfield County; possibly even to my ancestors Captain W.W.T. Cogbill who died fighting for the Confederacy in Pickett's Charge at Gettysburg, or Marcus Aurelius "Mac" Cogbill who carried the flag there and lived, only to have his eye shot out at Drewry's Bluff.

I suppose there is no avoiding the consequences of our choices. W.W.T. had an older brother named Charles Christian, a godless man who was arrested for forgery, escaped an insane asylum and disappeared, allegedly to Texas, to live under an assumed name. I hear rumors he did sire a large family, but if he ever saw his parents or brother again, I have not heard tell of it. The bill always comes due, in the end.

Ruth put a ham and turkey club in front of me and set about wiping down the counter. A man in a straw porkpie hat with a wide band and the brim turned down in front like Mickey Mouse in his traveling clothes lit up a cigarette and held two paper envelopes of sugar between his knuckles, shook them vigorously, tore off the ends, and emptied them into his coffee.

"How 'bout that business out at the Beach?"

"Wasn't that something? Just awful."

The man in the hat chuckled. "Come on, it was always a den of sin."

Ruth looked up from tidying the counter. "But a knife murder? That's a new kind of bad."

I put my sandwich down.

"I'm sorry, I didn't mean to eavesdrop. Knife murder?"

"You didn't hear?"

"I've been a little preoccupied."

"Fella was stabbed to death by some colored boy down by the pier."

"Anyone know who it was?"

"Sure, his family saw the whole thing." He pulled the front page of the paper out from under the pile and dropped it on top of the classifieds. The victim was named George Siever. He was a builder who was working on the Cloverdale project in Dahlgren. Witnesses identified the killer as twenty-five year old William Johnson. My helper back at Horne's. He was still at large. My heart sank. There had to be some mistake.

William was a good man, a hard worker. I couldn't figure why he would have done it.

I left a stack of bills on the counter and got out of there. I made my way back toward the courthouse and the sheriff's office in the new wing. The Aermotor behind Trinity church was ginning, a clattering that once signaled the drawing of water from a hand-dug well owned by the Morrises supplying the entire courthouse corridor.

There was a coffee cup on Powell's desk and a thick caramel odor in the air.

"Cogbill, how's that wife a yours?"

"William Johnson didn't stab that man."

"Why do I get the feeling you're into things that don't concern you?"

"I know William, we worked together. He's not the type."

"Well now, that idn't what six witnesses told the police in Colonial Beach. Was you there?"

"I'm not into anything yet, Sheriff."

"I note your use of the word 'yet'."

"I want to help you find him."

"You idn't authorized to do any such thing, Cogbill, and in case you forgotten that boy got a knife and a disposition for perforatin' caucasian fellers."

"Not the man I worked with. No sir."

"You never act one way at work and another way on your own time?"

"Not really, no."

"No wonder you cain't keep your situation. You need a ride or anything?"

"What I need is a job."

"Well don't look at me."

"I wasn't about to."

"You know Vee Clare?"

"I know the name." He owned several businesses in the county.

"Talk to him. He's a good feller and he's always looking for help."

"Suppose I might."

"And stay away from that Johnson boy."

I couldn't leave it alone. I drove to Port Royal, hoping I could talk Murray into giving me William's address. Maybe he had family I could talk to. Neighbors. Anybody who could give me the side of the story the papers wouldn't.

At the northeast corner of Route 17 and 301 in Port Royal was Brown's Motel, and on the southeast corner was Horne's, the yellow roof and red oval sign shining in the autumn sun. I parked nose in on the Route 17 side, where the roof overhung the sidewalk, the candy shop beyond plate glass windows.

Murray was not feeling charitable. In fact he was not feeling hospitable, at least not toward guys who'd lately made him eat his apron. The bruises on his face were fading but there was tape on his nose.

"You get outta here, Cogbill, I'll call the law."

"I'm not here to fight, Murray."

"You ain't getting no job back, neither."

"Don't want it. You heard about William?"

"Yeah I heard."

"I need his address."

"You know I can't give it to you."

"I'll just sit at the counter and have a milkshake while we wait on the law. Your customers'll enjoy watching a guy get arrested, right? Maybe I'll resist. Some stuff may get broken."

"You know, I never did like you."

"Hiya Harry."

"Hey Linda."

"Don't serve him! Don't you serve him!"

I was outside, watching a guy wrestling his wife's overstuffed suitcase in front of Brown's, when Linda the waitress came out the back door, struggling to keep her hair out of her face as she lit a cigarette.

"You're looking for William's address?"

"Yep."

"You know he ain't home, right? He killed a guy out at the Beach."

"It's got to be a mistake. They're blaming him because he's black. That's got to be it."

"Well either way he ain't home."

"I know."

She pushed her hair back again, and I noted the ash on the collar of her uniform and on her apron, and the tired, creased look of her skin that heavy smokers seemed to develop in their thirties. She'd tried to cover it with a thick layer of makeup that somehow only accentuated the creases at the corners of her mouth and the circles under her eyes.

"You know where Nanzatico is?"

Back across the James Madison Bridge in King George, I turned off 301 onto Salem Church Road, a narrow country lane that led past gates for plantations with names like Woodlawn and Oakenbrow, to a place called Welcome, in country so pure the trees seemed to resent human activity. On a rise beside the narrow road stood a small red-brick Baptist church called Salem, with an octagonal steeple, each face gabled beneath the spire, creating an unusual crown effect. The face of the church was flat, the door surrounded by six windows of various sizes. A few small homes sat huddled in fields, roofs of tin or tarpaper, roads unpaved and so narrow I would have to pull over should a vehicle approach from the opposite direction.

A short distance past the church, I turned off onto Nanzatico Lane in the shadow of a big gnarled oak. A red-tailed hawk watched me pass, then took to wing and flew above my car, like an ancient spirit guiding me into the previous century. The lane hedged along a hillside above the broad fields of Oakenbrow farm, jogged a couple of times between hills, and cut straight on through a sea of corn stubble toward Nanzatico Bay. At the end of the narrow dirt lane stood a cluster of magnolias and weeping willows, and looming among them the broad white face, mossy, hipped roof and towering chimneys of Nanzatico house stood watch beside the glistening gold of the bay.

The long, ochre-colored drive forked three ways before the stately trees, the center path passing through a low gate and terminating in a neat circle in front of the house. To the left stood a low barn, and a couple of simple cottages that had once been slave quarters. I pulled left at the fork, around the barn, and up to a shotgun house with a covered porch. A white-haired black man in a t-shirt and suspenders, his right arm missing below the elbow, sat in a rocking chair on the porch. His face looked as if it had been hewn from mahogany with a dull chisel.

He watched intently as I parked in front, then stood up from his chair and started inside.

"Sir!"

He stopped, and turned back to face me as I stood watching over the hood of the car.

"Don't want no trouble, no sir."

"Me neither. I'm a friend of William's."

"Don't William got no friends no mo'."

"He's got at least one."

"How I know you ain't a cop?"

"Well, I can show you some ID. But you can tell from the car I'm not a State Trooper and you know Powell's got no deputy."

He considered this a moment, nodded.

"Well if you gone show me some ID, reckon I luke at it."

I got my wallet out, and came around the car to the porch, handed it to him.

"Hay-ronimus Cogbill, Gera Road. How you know William from?"

"My friends call me Harry." He handed me back my wallet and I put it away. "I used to work at Horne's."

He nodded. "He were doing all right there, saving money."

"He's a good man," I said. "I don't believe the official story."

He didn't reply. His mouth turned down a little at the corners, and he squinted as he looked off across the fields of corn stubble.

"Know why they call this here place Nanzatico?"

I did not, and I shook my head by way of reply.

"Injuns lived here. Had they town right along here, they was fishers, mainly, and farmers, bowhunters you know. Now the white man had done drove a bunch of the tribes out they land so he could farm it for hisself. And the tribes fight each other sometime for land and for sport. So this Injun town, the Nanzaticos, they was all that was left of maybe four or five bands, Portabagos, Patowomecks, Matchotics. Was the early 1700's, they had papers saying they owned this land and could be here free and clear.

"But the white man, see, he want land. Always want land. And them Injuns was getting they toes stomped all over, so they went to the gubmint said they was tired of it. But ain't nothing happen, so you know what they did, sir?"

"I can guess."

"What any man do when don't nobody listen to him. They went to war. Kilt theyselves some white folks, and was hunted down and kilt by the white man's gubmint. Whatever was left, kids mainly, was taken for slaves."

I felt sick. "Why did you tell me that story?"

"William done what he done, Mr. Cogbill. Don't nobody care why."

I was driving back toward the lane when a man in a necktie and a starched white shirt stepped out into the drive and flagged me down. He had on a shooting vest and a pair of wool trousers, and a panama hat. There was a shotgun balanced on his shoulder, the stock cupped in his hand. He had a gold watch, an outdoorsman's tan, and crows feet at the corners of hazel eyes. He was fair-haired, tall and stocky, and had a jawline that was a little too round to be handsome.

I stopped and he came over to my window.

"You're not bothering my tenants, are you?"

"No sir."

"Got to make sure. Old Micah's polite but he's been leaned on pretty hard since his boy got hisself in trouble."

"And you are...?"

"Oh. Sorry. Tom Boone." He stuck his hand out and we shook briefly. His grip was firm and meaty, the backs of his knuckles coated in blond hairs. "You a cop, or...?"

"Nope, just a friend of the family."

"Funny I don't recognize you."

"I used to work with William."

Boone nodded and looked back toward Micah Johnson's house.

"Damn shame about Willy. I guess you never do know about anybody, especially coloreds."

I felt like bleaching my hand. Or maybe sawing it off at the wrist.

"What's different about black people, Mr. Boone?"

"Some things only the Lord truly understands. What did you say your name was?"

"Cogbill."

He almost did it. There was just the slightest tell that he knew my name, a twitch in the corner of his eye, but he covered it well.

"You still at Horne's?"

"No."

"Looking for work? I'm sure I can put the word out with some of my friends."

"That won't be necessary, Mr. Boone. Thanks."

"Well if you change your mind..."

"Sure thing." I threw it in gear and he stepped back to let me go. I wondered if Tom Boone might be L. Thomas Boone, a name I'd run across in the land records on the Cloverdale thing the year before. I drove back out to Salem Church Road thinking about Micah's story, the Nanzatico Indians fighting for their land, and I wondered at the way two and a half centuries could pass and yet so little change.

"Kenny'll butcher the hog tomorrow, I'll pick it up after lunch."

Outside it was raining again, and in truth I half hoped the rain would persist and wash away all thought of a barbecue.

"Great, we can have a Harry Got Fired party. Invite your daddy, he'll want a piece of that action."

I'd meant it as a joke but as the words came out my mouth I realized they, and the tone, were all wrong.

"I just want to have company, Cogbill. People are starting t' think we don't like them. I mean it'll just be Mildred and Dane Harris. Maybe Mr. and Mrs. Taylor, I know you like Elijah."

"You think they'll come?"

"Won't know 'til you ask them, will you?"

"That it, just those four?"

"Oh, I don't know! You have to invite more than you want because they won't all come. Maybe Gene and Freda, or you know Sarah and Jimmy."

I liked Gene and Freda. I liked them all. I couldn't explain why I was so terrified to be around good people. How could I make anyone understand? The one person in the world who knew my heart didn't even understand it. All at once outside the rain ceased and the sky grew cautiously bright.

In the kitchen I emptied a bottle of White House vinegar into a saucepan and cranked up the dial. Ethel came out to the kitchen and poured herself a glass of wine. I wanted to yank on the tie at her waist like the ribbon on a Christmas gift, to slide the robe back off her shoulders and kiss her neck and reestablish that sacred connection that had made the last year the best of my life, but I knew this was exactly wrong; a sort of Ethel-as-savior dynamic that would make her feel pressured and possessed at a time when she was already angry with me. It would be nothing short of a sabotage. Love is not like a movie, and do not let anybody tell you it is.

When the vinegar began to boil I stirred in Domino brand light brown sugar, and CF Sauer's mustard powder, black and red pepper, and garlic and onion powder. I stirred it until the sugar and the mustard powder dissolved, then set the pot aside to cool.

We barely spoke to each other for the rest of the evening. That night when she came to bed, she turned her back to me, barely glancing my way when she said goodnight and clicked off her lamp. As my eyes adjusted, I placed my hand on the swell of her hip under the blanket, and felt the soft warmth of her skin, but she pulled the covers tighter around her shoulders and did not face me.

Shadows danced like smoky wraiths above the bed, the hammering in my head like the forge of Hephaestus. My hands began to shake. A singularity opened in my chest and I could feel my happiness, my soul, the whole of what I had built with Ethel slowly sliding into it, never to return. At last I threw off the covers and stumbled into the living room.

The sound of wet lips smacked obscenely at my ear, and for just an instant I thought I saw the blue face of Nestor Lazos grinning in the corner near Ethel's bookshelf. When I turned on the light he was gone. Lazos was a Philadelphia button-man who had once paid us a visit when I annoyed some of his associates. Last year Ethel had emptied both barrels of her shotgun into Lazos' chest, pointblank in this very room. If you knew where to look the brown stains of his blood still lingered in the grain of the hardwood. I wrapped an afghan around myself, laid down on the sofa, and stared at the ceiling until the dull grey light of dawn filled the room like dirty cotton.

I am sure that in another life I may have been a knight and Ethel the lady in whose name and for whose honor I fought, and I wondered if I had failed her then as well. I imagined I had. In those ash-filled days of cookfires and plague-ridden towns whose street-side gutters overflowed with human excrement and the bodies of the dead, there had been only failure, for death came if not by consumption then by the sword. All in all I could not say the world had changed.

CHAPTER THREE

I DROVE UP to see the Taylors the next afternoon. Although I knew them fairly well at this point and there was nothing to be nervous about, my stomach pitched and roiled, and my bowels felt watery. I did not want to have a party, and it did not matter who was there. Instead of driving immediately up to the Taylors' house, I followed Dahlgren Road the rest of the way downhill to 301 at an uncontrolled intersection at the base of a sort of crater, and turned north.

The whole area was a low, marshy bog that stank like dead fish in summer, bifurcated by a two-lane highway that crossed a truss bridge over the Potomac into Charles County Maryland at a place called Morgantown. Ahead to the left, behind a small filling station, was what remained of the grass airstrip that had once belonged to Ethel's grandparents Jim and Vashti, and her Uncle Jack.

Near the middle of the old airfield a well, pump, and storage tanks were being constructed for the King George County Service Authority, and beside the creekbed toward the back corner where the two runways once met, a wastewater lagoon system was being excavated. Out near the highway, the ground was torn up and a well-worn swath of yellow dirt indicated the start of Danube Drive on what had been the main runway. A short distance in, the right-of-way for the first side street, Baltic Place, had been cleared and three model homes for the Cloverdale

Subdivision were under construction on a cul-de-sac near the bank of Williams Creek.

I parked on the still-gestating Baltic Place and walked across the bulldozer tracks in the yellow clay, following the sounds of hammering and power saws. The foreman was a little guy, maybe five-six, if I'm feeling generous. He was blond-haired and had sloping shoulders, corded forearms and a prominent Adam's apple. He had well-worn leather work gloves and a low-slung toolbelt.

"C'n I help you?"

"I don't know, I'm looking for George Siever."

"Siever's boys're off the project. Some kind of accident."

"That's too bad. Tom didn't mention it."

"Well that don't make much sense. Tom's the one pulled some strings to get us out here so fast."

"We're talking about the same Tom?"

"Boone. Leslie Thomas."

"Son of a bitch, that's the one. I must've got mixed up. What happened to George?"

"Nothing I want to talk about. You don't read the papers, do you?"

"It's too depressing."

"No shit, chief. So was that it?"

"I guess it was."

Off Owens Drive, in a neatly mown lawn with a tidy field full of tomato plants, squash bushes, and fat watermelons on the vine, sat a crooked little house with a bowed gallery and a stove-pipe chimney. The wood siding had been repainted in the spring, and the tin roof too, but already some rust was trying to show through.

Iris Taylor was out in the field with her basket, wearing wash-faded jeans scissored off at the ankles, a shirt that might have belonged to her husband, and a pair of sandals. A straw fedora was tied down on her head with a scarf and her shoulders were slightly hunched from years of working the field. She saw me and lifted a strong brown arm in the air, palm open by way of greeting.

Ethel was right that I liked the Taylors. It was their son who had saved my life in Europe, but it had come at the cost of his own and no matter how I tried, I always felt guilty in their presence.

"Mr. Harry, I'm sure glad you stopped by, can I get you something to drink? We got sweet tea and beer, or either I can make coffee."

"Now Mrs. Taylor I told you not to call me mister. I'm your son's age, I'm just Harry. And I don't want you to go to any trouble on my account."

Inside the house was full of cigarette smoke and the radio was on, Johnny Cash singing "Five Feet High and Rising." I could see the top of Elijah Taylor's head over the back of his favorite chair. He had a cigarette in an ashtray on a small side table among the smoldering remains of its brethren, and a glass of beer with ice cubes in it. He was the only man I ever knew who drank it that way.

"Taylor, Mr. Harry's here."

"'Ronymus come 'round where I can see you, you know I ain't gettin' out this chair."

His voice was gruff but full of humor. He worked overnight stocking shelves at the commissary on base, then pulled crab pots in the river at sunrise, before coming home and helping Iris in the garden in the morning. He slept the middle part of the day and was saving his energy to do it all over again that night. The Taylors were in their sixties, at least, and maybe more; Rollie had not been their oldest child and he would be my age; I was forty-one.

I came around and shook his hand, then retreated from the acrid cloud of smoke to a nearby seat.

"Hello Mr. Taylor, how you doing?"

"Old, tired, and more tired."

"And on'ry," Mrs. Taylor said.

"Ain't nobody ask 'bout you," he growled over his shoulder with a grin, and winked at me.

"He say he got a message from Miss Ethel."

"We're having a get-together on Saturday, just some friends, and we hoped you'd be able to come."

Taylor laughed.

"It's a barbecue," I said.

"Any other black folks gone be there?"

"I don't know."

"'Ronymus don't take it personal but I don't b'lieve we be welcome 'mong them folks."

"Well it's not—" I nearly said it's not a Klan rally but the words caught in my throat. "Do you think Ethel's friends would object to you?"

"Cogbill, if I ain't like you I be happy come fuck up your evening."

I grinned sadly. I didn't really blame him, but I was disappointed.

"Something else on your mind."

"It's like I'm going backwards, Pops. A friend of mine's in some trouble. I don't know if I can help him. They say he killed a man at the beach."

"That Johnson boy in the papers."

"I went out to his house, talked to his father."

"Tell you he ain't did it?"

"No. He told me he did. But there was something else. The man he killed, he worked for their landlord."

"You still on that Cloverdale thing."

"I don't know why these people don't just leave us alone."

"Sure you do, 'Ronymus. What we got in the county?"

"Mostly skunks and old houses."

"Land, boy. Land."

He had a point. Once it was all a huge plantation called Cleve, where Charles Carter made the first internationally recognized wine in the New World. It had just spent a couple of centuries getting divided again and again into smaller plots. At the rate we were going, they'd all be living in outhouses by the year 2000.

"Know why my house look this way?"

"What way? It's a fine house."

"Boy it's crookeder'n shit, and you know it."

His eyes took on that intensity that Rollie called "The Look," that once telegraphed to his children a strap was inbound.

"Okay, it's crooked."

"My daddy use't trap muskrats. Grew him some chickens. That was 'fore the Navy moved us out."

"The Navy moved you?"

"Moved the whole damn lot of us."

"Your family?"

"The whole community, Cogbill. So they build the base. Them that could, like Pop, moved they houses. The others packed up they shit and the man burned the houses down."

"Who gave them permission to do that?"

"Pres'dent Wood-drow Wilson."

I took 301 home and swung by the little clapboard store in Gera to pick up our mail. I bought a newspaper and an RC Cola, and watched John punch in the prices on the big brass register.

"Say, there was some kinda Yankee in here asking after you earlier."

"Christ, it wasn't an Italian guy by any chance? New York accent?"

"That's him."

"Tell me you didn't give my address."

"He said he was a friend of yours."

"Yeah, he's been laboring under that impression."

"Still got that grey fox?"

"Yep. Wrecks the house, but Ethel likes him."

John just smiled and shook his head as he made change.

"Say, I don't want to touch any tender spots, but could you maybe ask your father-in-law to come pick up his mail?"

"He hasn't been in?"

"Not for months. If I give it to you, will you see it gets to him?"

I drove out to the Burkitt place, and up the long driveway flanked by tin-capped fence posts. I hadn't been out there since Ethel had moved in with me the year before, and I was shocked at the change. The fields were overgrown, the porch was being slowly pulled apart by vines, and a shutter had broken loose on one of the upstairs windows. A fish crow sat on the tail of the big Aermotor behind the house, awping as I got out of the car.

I had a box full of mail for Frank, and I carried it on my hip. The porch looked like a piano where the keys were going flat. I pounded on the door and waited a long moment until I heard something falling over inside, and the wraith of Frank Burkitt appeared at the door.

"What are you doing here?"

There was such venom in the way he said it, I considered heaving the box of mail at his feet and stalking back to my car, but despite the tension that had existed between Frank and me since I first began dating his daughter, I now felt a great swell of pity for the man.

"John wanted to make sure you got your mail."

"Get out of here."

"Your mail, Frank."

"Leave it and go."

"We're having a party tonight. Ethel would probably like it if you came."

"Don't tell me what she'd like. Don't say her name."

"I'd think you'd want to see her happy."

"I would. Why I'm not coming. She thinks she's happy but she ain't, or she won't be for long. You're nothing, Cogbill. You ever tell her about your Army record?"

"About Rollie Taylor? Yes."

"About the rest of it. The boy and his mother. The fight that ended your time in the service. She know about that?"

I felt the harpsicord strings in my skull winding tighter.

"She don't, I can see it in your face."

In my mind, I could see myself smashing through his stormdoor, beating the little gremlin that had once been Franklin Burkitt until whatever was left looked like the floor of a slaughterhouse.

Instead I dropped the box of mail on his porch and stepped down to the clay and started for my car. But before I got far I turned back to him.

"You know what I think, Frank? I think you need to let her go. She's not a child. You don't own her."

"You son of a bitch."

"Be the man she needs you to be."

As I drove away, I wondered to whom I was speaking: Frank, or me.

The man who butchered Frank's hog had done a perfect job of it. We got a whole cooler full of packages of various sizes containing jowls, ham hocks, fatback, ham, bacon; loins and shoulders for the barbecue, and even the ears to give Fawkes.

It was late morning, and the sun was high enough the shadows were short and dark, dragonflies glittering like red and green jewels as they darted around the field. I was wearing an old work shirt and dungarees I kept for poking around the yard. I added charcoal and split chunks of hardwood to the shallow, gravel-filled pit. A can of lighter fluid popped and rang in my hand as I squeezed enough out onto the coals and the chunks of wood, and lit the fire with a wooden kitchen match.

The heat shimmered the air above the pit, and the smell of the butane gave way to that of burning coal and wood, and when the temperature was right I placed a grille over the pit and laid the pork butts out, glistening with brown sauce, and covered them with a large clay pot. It was going to take six to eight hours to cook through. I lifted off the wide-brimmed, silver belly hat I was wearing, the crown telescoped and almonded, a birthday gift from Ethel, and mopped my brow with a kerchief. I ran it around the leather band inside the hat as well, then screwed the hat down low on my head and stuffed the kerchief back in my pocket.

Ethel was in the kitchen grating fresh cabbage from the garden – the slaw was her recipe – and we had several bags of hamburger buns from the Circle Market. There were a couple cases of Northern Neck Ginger Ale, Coca-Cola in green glass contour bottles, and tins of potato chips, and in a while I'd make beans, then run out and buy ice to fill the cooler.

"Meat's on."

"Good. I told everybody it'd be okay if they show up about four-thirty but I wouldn't mind if they come earlier."

"Yeah," I said. "That way you won't have to talk to me."

She stopped with the cabbage and I thought for an instant flames were going to shoot out of her eyes.

"Hieronymus..."

"You're angry with me."

"Well I am NOW."

"I'm sorry, Ethel."

"Are you? Take a good look at yourself, Cogbill. Anything you build you have to tear it down. You're trying to ruin this marriage so you can set around feel sorry for yourself."

"I couldn't go back to that."

"Then stop trying to. I am confused as hell about why you have to act this way. I'm a little angry that you'd say such a damned fool thing, and yes, I am disappointed that you got yourself fired. But don't you dare for one second act like I don't love you."

"The other night..."

"Well I didn't make you sleep on the couch, you know."

"I didn't exactly feel welcome in bed."

"Making love don't magically make everything better."

"I know that."

"I still sleep better with you beside me."

"Me too."

"So ask yourself what do you want. You keep working these simple jobs, you don't think there's more to you than flipping burgers or mopping floors?"

"I guess I'm sort of unilaterally bad at everything."

"No you're not. You're a good cook, but that ain't what you really love. Figure out what God put in your heart, Cogbill."

I thought she had more to say, but there was a knock at the door.

"That cain't be one of our friends already."

"If it's Joey DeLarosa you may hear some crying."

But it wasn't gimpy Joey standing on the gallery.

"Hello Mr. Cogbill, forgive the intrusion." He was wearing a pair of Ray-Ban Clubmaster sunglasses and a golf shirt and chinos, but I recognized the man with the scar in his eyebrow from my last day at Horne's.

"What are you doing at my house?"

"Hey now, let's be cool. I got your address from the guy at the country store. I just come with a warning, is all."

"Don't come near my home again."

"I'm an attorney. Hector Adagio. I had a couple questions about your friend Joey."

"He's not my friend."

"Good. Because he's not who you think he is."

"I'm sorry, don't you guys usually hire private investigators to do all the, ah, investigating?"

"I'm not licensed to practice law in the Commonwealth of Virginia, Mr. Cogbill. I'm down here on other business. But your Joey is a person of interest in a case my office is working on. Just stay clear of him, okay? It's not something you want to drag your family into."

"I haven't seen him. Mr. Adagio. I don't like him. He's a pain in the ass."

"That is undeniably true. All the same, here's my card. If he should try to contact you, call my answering service."

The card had addresses for Brooklyn, Palm Beach, Kansas City, and Los Angeles. A sick feeling bubbled up in my stomach. When I turned my eyes back up to meet his, the look on his face was like a tiger about to pounce.

"Mr. Adagio, I'd like you to leave now."

"Don't lose my number, Mr. Cogbill."

He turned and stepped down off my porch toward a gleaming Lincoln Continental like a black shark circling in the yellow clay of my driveway.

Ethel stepped up behind me, wiping her hands on her apron.

"Who was that?"

"Trouble."

Although I hoped that would be the end of it, I knew even then it wasn't. The energy around us had shifted. I rather had the feeling of a car barrel-rolling down a mountain; parts were pinwheeling through the air, the chrome was busted loose, and shards of glass swirled, refracting the sunlight, beautiful and deadly. I could not fight the cosmic arm that drove that tumbling catastrophe.

That evening as a million cicadas rattled in the trees, the sound rippling across the open air like rings on the surface of a lake, I watched a tom turkey and his harem rooting for snails in the field. Millie, Sarah, and Freda were sitting with Ethel in the yard near the house, the lowering sun haloing her hair. Millie was tall and moon-faced, her dark hair piled atop her head; she wore a pair of catseye glasses. Freda was Gene's wife, fair-haired and bright-eyed. Sarah was short and plump, round face framed with curled red hair that made her look like old-fashioned folk art of a smiling sun.

I watched Ethel laughing and picking at her barbecue, in a blue dress that brought out the color of her eyes, and although I knew I should delight in her happiness I wondered how she could laugh and smile as though nothing were wrong. Near me, Jimmie and Dane were drinking Cokes and holding paper plates with barbecue sandwiches, squinting against the golden light. Dane was bald, with a fringe of dark hair and sideburns, and a pair of thick glasses that made his eyes seem too small for his face. Jimmie's head was square and his wavy hair was swept back, and there was a blotch of slaw on his chin.

For my part I was trying to remember why I knew the name Hector Adagio. No matter how I pushed, I kept hitting a wall. I became aware, slowly, that Gene was talking, and then that he was talking to me. He was a tall, rangy guy with dark hair, narrow features and a thin line of a mouth.

"Said that sauce is pretty good."

"Mmm," I said, half-listening. How could I talk about sauce when my world was crumbling?

"Say you make that yourself?"

"Yep, that's my recipe."

Gene worked as a financial advisor on base. He was also a volunteer firefighter and played on the firefighters' sandlot baseball team.

"Pig come from old Frank's place?"

"That's right."

"Maybe you're growing on him."

The turkeys flew into the treeline at the edge of my property.

"Eh?"

"Said maybe you're growing on him."

"I doubt it."

Just beyond the edge of the forest I thought I saw a shadow move. I tried to focus: it could be Adagio, or my imagination, but I thought it had been a young black man in dark clothing. Sometimes I was visited by the shade of Rollie Taylor; I was never sure if he was real or a creation of my guilty conscience.

Another round of laughter from Ethel and her friends.

"You seem distracted."

"What's that?"

"Said you seem distracted."

"I'm sorry," I said. "I don't really know what I'm doing here."

Gene rejoined Dane and Jimmie, leaving me with my thoughts. I regretted being rude to Gene. He was a good guy and I liked him, but I couldn't pretend I was having a good time. Dane Harris looked as uncomfortable as I felt. His mouth was compressed to a tight little line, his eyes darting around as if looking for an exit. He approached me with a slight grin that didn't extend to his eyes.

"You plant all those flowers?" he said.

"Those are wildflowers."

Our fields were spattered with color: yellow asters and black-eyed susans, wild marigold, daisy-like chamomile, and fuzzy purple clusters of nodding thistle, all swarming with tiger swallowtails. The fences were draped in tendrils of wild grape and five-leafed Virginia creeper. In places trees were appearing, elm and poplar, and white cedars with their horned blue berries, as unavoidable in King George County as grackles in spring.

"So they more or less just grow there?"

"Yeah Dane, that's...that's how that works."

"Did you ever farm it?"

"Somebody did, but that was before my time. If it wasn't for Ethel I probably wouldn't have a backyard."

I wished I had some paint to watch dry. Another minute of this and my ghost was going to jump out and float away from sheer boredom. Dane threw out his plate, the last of his sandwich held in his hand.

"Gotta keep the little woman happy," he said, grinning suddenly, trying to intimate sympathy. His lips curled in like a chimp when he smiled.

"I don't call her that," I said.

"Look at the time, you want a Coke?" He put his hands in his pockets, evidently forgetting he was still holding part of a sandwich, and blithely strolled away toward the bucket of ice, a stain slowly spreading on his hip.

I heard Millie exclaim, "Oh Dane, what's in your pocket?"

"I wish you hadn't pointed that out."

"Well the whole world can see it. I just washed those!"

"Do we have to do this right now?"

"You're the one putting food in your pocket."

"I can get y'all a towel."

"Now don't go to any trouble Ethel, it's his own fault. I swear he embarrasses me every time we go out."

"I embarrass you? You treat me like a child!"

"Well you ACT like a child, Dane!"

Jesus Christ. I drifted around the yard, checking the food in Fawkes' pen, and studying the bands of pink and blue above the rustling treetops in the long, lazy shafts of the sinking sun. I wanted to find a hole and crawl in it until the awkwardness was over, which I figured ought to be right around the time the sun exploded. I was out front when Ethel came onto the porch squinting in the evening sun.

"What are you doing? We have guests."

"This exhausts me, Ethel."

"You're exhausting, Cogbill. You're like a bottomless pit of exhaustion. If I ain't tired, five minutes with you usually does the trick."

"Well I'll just go right to hell, then."

She caught up to me as I was climbing in my red-and-black Ford Crestline.

"Cogbill, wait."

I started the engine and killed the parking brake.

"Hieronymus!"

I left her standing in the orange driveway, arm shading her eyes, blue dress swaying slightly in the breeze. It was as though the awkwardness of the gathering had infected me, or maybe it was I who had caused the awkwardness to start with. I was never sure; the energy of those around me and that of my own soul were always difficult to distinguish. In the moment I felt only an instinctual desire to get away.

I drove without purpose, from Gera down the sharp little hill to Millbank Road, first Faron Young and then Jimmy Dean on the radio. I made a right at White's Corner, past the horses in the pasture and the old caretaker's house to Powhatan Plantation, the home of former US Ambassador to Ireland and famed horse breeder Raymond R. Guest, the mansion a brick beauty crouched atop its green hill. Kitty Wells and then George Jones as I swung left onto Port Conway Road at the rather dangerous intersection among the trees at Dogue.

There was a little store on the corner at the road to Cleve, a dusty country road that led past Berry Plain out to where Charles Carter's estate had once been. Out here it always felt as if the hills remembered the feudal lords in their mansions, presiding over miles of crops farmed on the bent backs of slaves trafficked in from Africa through the Caribbean, the young forests shouldering the blacktop nourished by the blood that saturated the knurled earth and gave the very clay its color.

On the radio the DJ gave us Patsy Cline's new single, "Crazy," a Willie Nelson cover that I thought she'd improved upon greatly. The song, a slow, tinkly, lonesome affair about being brokenhearted and blaming oneself for attachment, must have hit a little too close to home, because I was pretty far into my feelings when the accident occurred.

I admit that I was not attentive to my speed, but the green beetle of a Chevy that came whipping around the bend from the direction of Port Conway was way over the center line, and I jerked the wheel, stomped the brake, and felt the big Ford get away from me as her ass kicked out and the front end swung toward the trees. The car bucked viciously, less automobile than angry bull, and absurdly in that moment I remembered a story Rollie had once told me about a young corporal who wrecked a motorcycle after a night of heavy drinking. He'd walked away without injury because his drunkenness had relaxed his muscles. The world was a green and gold blur. I let go of the steering wheel, let my arms hang limp at my sides, and clenched my face like a fist.

CHAPTER FOUR

THE SUNLIGHT dripped through the canopy like molten glass and turned the leaf-papered ground to fire where it struck. A clear stream tinkled over moss-shrouded stones and somewhere above, in the distant gothic arches of the forest ceiling, a pileated woodpecker laughed like an old woman deep in her cups.

My feet carried me through holly, greenbrier, and running cedar, among ash and sweet gum tethered to the earth by wild grape, following the scent of wood smoke and roasted fish until in a neat clearing I entered a carefully ordered village of long-houses lashed with woven mats, where tall, raven-haired men in little more than their own cinnamon-hued skin squatted on their haunches sharpening stone projectile points, their scalps shorn to stubble above the ears.

No one spoke to me or acknowledged my presence; in any case I did not speak Virginia Algonquian. Ash from cookfires drifted like snow on the breeze, lifting and falling, lifting again; strong, tattooed women with nothing but deerskin aprons at their waists gathered vegetables from gardens and sat in groups beading leggings and moccasins.

I passed through the darkened entrance of a longhouse, where gar and sturgeon cooked on hearths down the center and smoke rolled lazily in pale sunbeams through exhaust holes in the roof. At the rear of the house, in a kind of shadowy loft, I could see through the smoke a few older men sharing a pipe.

One regarded me with sightless eyes, got the attention of one of his fellows, and pointed to me with his lips in a peculiar motion I had never seen before.

This second man, by his bearing the leader, motioned me in. I cautiously approached, not wishing to disrespect them or the home. As I squatted before him, I could see the red and blue beads cutting geometric patterns across the tapered toes of his slippers. From a large covered basket he presented me with a carved fox, the bracelets on his tattooed wrists clattering softly. I cradled the stone figure in my hands and looked into the chief's shadowed face.

"I don't understand."

He opened his mouth, and a glowing orb like a small sun hovered there, searing a turquoise disk into the back of my eyelids as I screwed them shut. When I tried to open them again, groaning, I was lying in the grass, the dream still pulsing like blood in my heart. My head quivered like a struck bell and meaning slipped, piscine, through my fumbling grasp.

I have come to believe that time is just the fourth dimension in space, and that our perception of it is due only to the limited capacity of the clumsy organisms we inhabit. I wasn't anywhere near the road or my car. All around me was a field, and a dark line of trees in the distance ahead of me. Even as I walked I was not sure if the year was 1960 or 1360. The landscape around me offered little in the way of clues, except that the fields in the gloaming of the day resolved themselves into the quilted countryside of the white man's world.

I saw a faint glimmer of light through the trees, and reoriented towards it. My head was killing me. Probing it with my fingers I could feel a swollen spot, tender and ringing with pain. Hadn't that been Joey DeLarosa's car that forced me off the road? Or was that part of the dream? I couldn't tell anymore. The fireflies were so thick in the fields and forests around me that I felt removed from reality entirely. The lights winked on and off in waves in the gathering darkness as far as I could see, a map of the cosmos sprawled across the countryside like a blanket of Christmas lights. Hell, maybe I'd died after all.

As I walked my vision dimmed and I must have slid out of full consciousness again; the night rushed on all at once like some divine hand twisting a dimmer. The moon sat low, fat and heavy, a baleful yellow eye wrapped in black velvet, turning the night air to gauze. A whippoorwill shrilled plaintively in the dark. The bugs were singing, rattling, trilling their nocturnal chorus.

High above me across the infinite wastes I could clearly see Orion, Ursa Major, and all the other constellations of the northern hemisphere, precious jewels spread upon a bed of deep indigo. A meteorite burned green and gold as it entered the atmosphere, breaking up into a trail of orange sparks fading from sight.

The landscape around me was desolate; I entered a road, little more than a muddy scar cut through weedy hills and fields, and passed along a churchyard bounded with a spindly iron fence. A large plantation house I did not recognize sat in a field in the middle distance. Around me now was a mostly abandoned village of little clapboard houses with high open gables and tall brick chimneys, some with crow-steps and draped with fishing nets; beyond them a darkly shimmering ribbon of water a mile wide. A black ferryman stood in a scow at a crooked wooden dock, buttoned into a canvas waistcoat and high-waisted trousers, tall pole in hand, as two men in dirty frock coats clambered aboard. One, a handsome fellow with a black slouch hat pulled low on his forehead and a couple weeks' growth of beard around a drooping moustache, had a bandaged hand and a swollen leg; he wore only one boot and sat a horse as he boarded the vessel in spite of the protestations of the ferryman.

His companion was a rough-looking man with an overbite and a broad face shaded by dark stubble, his lank oily hair falling across his temples, framing wide-set eyes. He had a carbine and wore a satchel across his shoulder. With them were three men in the mismatched grey uniforms of the Confederate Army, one carrying a pair of makeshift crutches. The travelers spoke to each other in hushed tones, and none but the ferryman gave any sign they saw me. This last, the black man in the canvas vest, looked directly at me with the same confusion I felt myself, for surely he was Jim Thornton, the man with the overbite Davy Herold, and his companion upon the horse John Wilkes Booth himself, heading for his doom at Garrett's Farm.

I startled out of the vision and found myself sitting in the dark on some kind of narrow bench, moonlight filtering eerily in strips through shuttered windows. I could see enough to recognize the sanctuary of a small church. Real or not, I no longer ventured to guess. I do not remember all the words I spoke to Him that night, and in any case most of them certainly did not bear repeating. But at last when I heard a door open behind me I didn't know whether to be hopeful or terrified.

Then the lights came on with a snap and from the blinding white a voice said, "Jesus, Cogbill." When the white broke up into colors and the pain in my optic nerves bled like smoke into ether, a blocky form resolved itself into Sheriff Jay Powell. "Your wife's about out of her mind."

The church had four gothic windows shuttered up tight, a floor of wide, even planks, and a burgundy runner up the aisle.

The light came from a single brass chandelier in the center of the little sanctuary. A narrow balcony above the door contained an ancient pipe organ.

"I need to report an accident."

Powell held a squat glass bottle out to me as we sat in the front of his cruiser, parked in the gravel loop in front of Emmanuel Church in Port Conway. The little brick church sat in a neat square yard, surrounded by a low brick wall with iron gates. The occasional flash of sheet-lightning inverted the night sky. The universe is infinite and its mysteries unfathomable, and I focused on the smell of the whiskey and the feel of the vinyl and bakelite and glass, to the tactile and familiar, and hoped to God I would not lose my grip upon it.

"You want to help me put a hurting on this old feller and maybe you get to feeling all right after while."

"You have a fifth of whiskey in your police car?"

"Well, it was a fifth this morning. Reckon it's still about enough to get the job done."

I wasn't much of a drinker, but it didn't seem like the time to refuse the offer. It smelled like caramel but tasted like spiced turpentine; at least it took the edge off the knot growing on my head.

"What, uh, was the occasion?"

"Ever'thin' okay?"

"I dunno, sheriff."

"Well that ain't an encouraging answer. Sure you don't want to go to the hospital?"

"I'm not even sure I want to go home."

"Miss Ethel's pretty worried."

"Reckon she's mostly just disappointed with her worthless husband." I passed him his bottle back.

"You ain't mess around on her, did you?"

"Sheriff what in the hell kind of...for God's sake, I love her. I would never."

"So what happened?"

"We were having a party."

"She wanted her friends over and you wadn't having a good time, there were a fight an' you left. That about right?" He took a swallow, passed the bottle back.

"Yeah, I reckon that says it."

"Cogb... Harry. Come on, hoss. It ain't a marriage in the world don't go through this stuff. You think the King of England don't have to put up with a buncha shit from the Queen?"

"There's no King of England," I said. "The Queen is the reigning monarch. If her husband was called King it would upset the balance of power. He's the Duke of Edinburgh."

"DUKE? Well that ol' boy's really screwed idn't he? I'll drive you home. Put the little woman's mind at ease. You want my advice, when you get home, get down on your knees, beg her to forgive you, and do whatever she says. And I by-God mean whatever she says, Cogbill."

I drank some more turpentine.

"One of the other couples started arguing, it was awful."

"That idn't on you."

"I embarrassed her in front of our friends."

"Well I don't know 'bout them Dahlgren types, but Gene ain't got a mean bone in his body. Him and Miss Freda won't hold it against you."

The country roads were empty under the stars, but with the windows down we could hear the ringing chorus of bugs and bullfrogs as we ripped along. I passed Powell his bottle again.

"What about my car?"

He waved his hand like he was swatting away a fly.

"We got a wrecker on it. You can call the shop on Monday and pass along your insurance information and whatnot."

"Thanks sheriff."

"Christ, I better slow down on the booze, I could swear I just heard you thank me."

"You know anything about a Hector Adagio?"

"Whatever you're doing, don't."

"So you know him."

"No I don't know him, but I know you, and if you're asking questions you're detectin' without a detectin' license, and that annoys me."

"Why?"

"I like to keep things simple."

"He's a lawyer, from New York. But he's been asking questions about this busboy from Horne's, Joey DeLarosa. Only he calls him Tony. Joey spooked when he saw Adagio at the restaurant, tore ass out of there. I think it was Joey's car that ran me off the road tonight."

"Don't go looking for trouble."

"Sheriff, I know the name Adagio, I've heard it before. I think it came up in the Pope's Field thing. With Jimmie Vasiliou and Nicky Drakos."

About a year ago I had gotten tangled up with some Greek mafia types down from Maryland who were the primaries on the real estate and construction project on the land that used to belong to Ethel's family. I never sorted the mess. I saw in the paper that the development had changed hands, but I'd stayed out of it, at least until I started asking about Siever and William Johnson. Ethel was safe and I cared about little else.

"That's over with. Let it go. Go make up with your wife."

We rumbled over the cattle guard and up into the turna-round in front of my house.

"I still don't have a job, Sheriff."

"You talk to Vee Clare yet?"

"Well, no. I've been kind of busy."

"Cogbill, now damn it, listen to me. Get your house in order and don't get distracted with what-all don't concern you. You hear me?"

"I hear you, Jay."

"Want me go to the porch wit' you, provide backup?"

"I don't know."

"Let's go, Cogbill. Come on." He got out of the car and so did I, and we walked together up the steps onto the wide gallery porch.

Ethel opened the door before we could knock, and stood there framed in the warm yellow light, in her bathrobe, holding it tight at her throat, and looked at me with wide blue eyes. Fawkes walked between her ankles and looked up at us, the hem of the robe draped across his silver head like a wimple.

"There were an accident Miss Ethel, no serious injuries. Cogbill here was attempting to walk home, but he got hisself turned around. Reckon he meant to be home some time ago. Says he don't want to go to the hospital but he got a big ol' knot on his head."

"I'm sorry I ruined the party," I said. "I'm an idiot."

"I was hurtful and I apologize. I know these things aren't easy for you. I know you'd do just about anything to make me happy."

"But I can't be anyone other than me. Sometimes I worry that isn't enough."

She leaned forward, arms at her sides, and buried her face in my chest. "Hieronymus I didn't marry anyone else."

I put my arms around her waist and clung to her like a drowning man. Her arms came up and circled my neck and pulled my head down to her.

"You two have a nice night," Powell said.

CHAPTER FIVE

SUNDAY MORNING I woke up sore, but the tenderness in my head had receded significantly. I downed a couple aspirin and we attended services at Trinity Methodist, a red-brick, tin-roofed church near the courthouse, with a big tree in the gravel lot in front, an Aermotor windmill in back, and a stained-glass image of Jesus praying in Gethsemane in the rose window below the steeple. Ethel drove us in her pickup.

The new pastor was named Arta Shomo, a former Republican member of the West Virginia House of Delegates, but that had been some forty years past. He was nearly 70 now, and likely nearing his retirement from the ministry. Our previous minister, Braxton Epps, had been reassigned to Shacklefords down in King and Queen County. Such is life in the Methodist Church.

After the service, Gene and Freda came and wished us a good morning.

"We were awful worried about you last night, Harry," Freda said.

"Could tell you was distracted," Gene said. "Good to see you made it home all right."

What do you say to a young couple who have the opportunity to dress you down and instead show you the face of God?

When Ethel and I got home we cleaned up the mess from the party, then packed some leftover barbecue and slaw, and a couple of Cokes, and walked out across our fields among grasshoppers and tiger swallowtails, to a quiet place we liked near the edge of the trees. I spread a blanket and we ate our lunch in the shade of a black walnut tree, listening to the drumming of a downy woodpecker and the hoarse mewling of a catbird.

After we ate, Ethel took off her clothes and stretched out on the blanket to take the sun. Her mere presence has always put me at a loss for words and altered the rhythm of my soul, irrespective of the passage of time or its effects on us both.

She pushed her sunglasses up in her hair and scrunched her eyes against the light when she looked at me.

"You given much thought to what you wanna do for work?"

I took off my shirt and laid out gingerly beside her, the compression in my ribs causing a momentary stab of pain. "I guess I'm going to hit the bricks again tomorrow."

"What gives you joy, Hieronymus? What can you see yourself gladly doing every day? I mean other than what I know's on your mind."

I wasn't sure I knew any joy apart from Ethel's company, and I said so. Something was poking me in the hip; I reached under the blanket and came up with a small carved figure. I wiped a little dirt off it with my thumb, placed it on my chest, and wondered not for the first time about the true nature of reality.

"You'll figure it out, I believe in you. Is that a fox?"

"Yep."

"Where'd it come from?"

I thought about the dream, a Virginia centuries-lost, and the chief with the sun in his mouth. But I had no explanation for the little carving that now rose and fell with every breath I took.

"I hit my head pretty hard."

She took the tiny stone fox off my chest and turned it over in her hand.

"It reminds me of the morning I found you both," I said.

"You're just a fool for lost people."

"Is Fawkes people?"

"Reckon he thinks so. Mainly I meant me."

"It wasn't you who was lost that morning, Ethel. It was me."

She replaced the carving on my chest, and we laid there that way while a red-tailed hawk soared overhead, and water babbled through a wash just inside the treeline. She looked at me with wide eyes, her front teeth resting gently on her lower lip.

"I know I told you the other night that making love don't make everything better," she said.

"You did."

"Didn't mean I don't sometimes enjoy it."

I guessed in retrospect that the clues had been difficult to miss. I kissed her, and fumbled out of the rest of my clothes, and made love to my wife beneath the sun and the sky, while a cicada rattled his wings in the tree above us, and the butterflies wandered lazily on the breeze, and the stress and worry and self-flagellation of the last few days rushed out of us, and our bodies melted together as if in answer to the Almighty hand that had joined our souls.

Afterward she nestled up under my arm and I held her until she fell asleep. I watched the way her breasts rose and fell as she breathed and her hair, still curled from church, fluttered in the breeze. I thought not for the first time or the last that I did not deserve her love, and that nothing less than God's mercy could have cemented my place in her life.

Later, as I stood at the kitchen sink cleaning up the stuff from the picnic, I heard Ethel scream from down the hall. I dropped everything and charged to her but didn't get far before

I heard a crash and a whiney male voice with a New York accent exclaim "Christ, I'm sorry!"

"Ethel are you--?"

Gimpy Joey was sprawled on the floor in the hallway with a cut on his cheek and a rapidly swelling eye. Ethel stood over him, red-faced, her lips twisted off to one side.

"You know this creep?"

"That's Joey DeLarosa. Did he hurt you?"

"Tha's your wife, Hare? Jesus, I think she broke my face."

"What the goddamned hell are you doing in my house, Joey?"

"Lookin' fa you. I got problems, awright? I don't like hanging my ass out on the porch. The door was unlocked."

"I don't know what they do in New York, mister, but down here we wait for an invite before we come in a body's house. Now get out."

"You heard the lady, Joey. You going or do I need to pitch you myself?"

"I need your help, Hare."

I grabbed him by his collar and hauled him to his feet.

"You almost killed me last night."

He seemed confused a moment. "Look, they're after me, okay?"

"Stay away from me, Joey. Whatever you're into, don't bring it here."

I steered him to the front door.

"I got nobody else to go to. Please, ya gotta help me."

"If you come near my wife again I'll kill you myself."

"I t'ought you was my friend."

"That's your problem, Joey. You don't understand basic kindness."

I threw him off the porch.

He got to his feet and hobbled across the yard. "Awright, Cogbill, you wanna be a dick about it. Just remember I tried ta warn you."

The green Chevy bottomed out crossing the cattle guard.

"I'm sorry, Ethel."

"It ain't your fault."

"I don't know what his problem is."

"He cain't tell where his business ends and other people's begins. Women see it all the time. Desperation."

I couldn't disagree. I had the uncomfortable feeling the reason I didn't like Joey was because deep down I worried what I saw when I looked at him was what others saw when they looked at me. Just as quickly as I thought it, I wrapped that feeling up like last week's chicken bones and buried it in my emotional wastebasket. I swallowed another couple aspirin and gave Fawkes his supper. I hoped I'd seen the last of Joey, and Adagio, and for that matter the black cloud that rolled into my soul like raw sewage into a clear stream every time some silly thing didn't go my way. But these thoughts were not realistic and the actions of other men beyond my control.

It was Saturday and a mild October day and Ethel and I were standing in the grass in front of the Courthouse in early afternoon, watching a convoy of Civil War themed floats pulled by pickup trucks and freshly-washed farm tractors crawling West on Route 3 as the King George Marching Foxes bomped out a disheveled tune, the trilling of flutes and the rattle of snares drifting away into the smell of exhaust and wood smoke. Antique cars and novelties and horse-drawn wagons crawled by; the Kilmarnock Rescue Squad, John J. Wright High School Marching

Band from Spotsylvania. There were equestrians and baton corps from the Fredericksburg VFW. Twenty-five contestants for Festival Queen smiled and waved from convertibles and floats.

The Shiloh PTA had a particularly impressive float depicting General Ambrose Burnside and his men crossing the Rappahannock to Fredericksburg. The Dahlgren Lions Club had a model of the CSS Virginia, the ironclad usually referred to as the Merrimack. There was a shooting demonstration by the 17th Virginia Infantry, and some seven-hundred pounds of barbecue that sold out before the day was over. Democratic Eighth District Congressman Howard W. Smith was the Parade Marshal. The Sheriff was there, and the Judge, and the farmers, and bankers, and their wives and sons and daughters, and the wind rattled the leaves and made the boughs creak in the oak trees in front of the red-brick, Queen Anne-style schoolhouse where the narrow two-lane traced a ridgeline from Saint Anthony of Padua Catholic Church to Willow Hill at Arnold's Corner.

I admit that I have never particularly understood what there is to celebrate about the arrival of autumn: the acrid scent of smoke, the pungent odor of decay, the wasting of flowers beneath the ashen sky, a bleak annual reminder of the groping hand of Death and the insidious encroachment of the grave. But perhaps that was the point; a rural, family-friendly mardi gras, a bit of lightness and laughter and sense of community to buoy the spirit in anticipation of the long dark of winter. I held Ethel's hand and saw Jay Powell eating a barbecue sandwich, shaking hands and slapping backs and tipping his hat to women and girls, and taking an obvious delight in the company of his neighbors and the pride of the community, and I wondered why the older I got the strongest feeling I had was of aloneness, and futility, as though somewhere far behind me I had missed a turn and pressed on stubbornly, roaring full-tilt toward the cliffs of my mortality.

Ethel, perhaps sensing my mood, let go my hand and grabbed my arm with both of hers, pressing it to her breasts. She laid her head up on my shoulder and squinted up at me in the sun.

"What's on your mind, Hieronymus?"

"Just wondering why the more I see people enjoying themselves, the more I keep seeing skulls and crossbones."

"You want to know what your problem is?" Whenever she asked me that I knew she was about to filet my guts, but it was one of the things I loved and respected her for.

"Sure, what the hell."

"You don't never allow yourself to exist in the moment, Cogbill. The closer people stand to you the farther away your mind goes."

"Not when it's you doing the standing."

"I can see through your bullshit, but that ain't the same thing. You worry endlessly about things you cain't control. Jesus himself says not to do that and yet here you are."

I didn't know how to respond. Everything was beautiful and so fleeting and impermanent and if I could preserve it all, exactly as it was, I would. But then it would not be living and growing and there could be neither beauty nor truth without the possibility of deceit or destruction. So we live each moment under the constant ticking of the clock and the creeping hand of cellular decay, each act of pleasure echoing the embrace of the Lovers of Pompeii.

"You're doing it now, Hieronymus."

I buried my face in her hair and took her in my arms and held her, and the moment snapped into focus and I saw the sunshine and felt the breeze and smelled the grass and the earth and the barbecue, and for a moment could almost remember the little boy that I had been three decades past, when each new day was an adventure that seemed to last a lifetime and the grim reaper owned no real estate in my consciousness.

"Sometimes I can't tell if I cling too tightly to things, or not tightly enough."

"Maybe it ain't how you cling, but what you cling to, Cogbill."

"Meaning what?"

"Meaning this moment is all we have. Right now. Not yesterday, and not tomorrow. Not five minutes in either direction. Just right now."

"Right now is pretty good."

"Right now is the best."

I kissed her and felt her body swell against me. My scalp tingled and my loins stirred and my arms and the back of my neck crackled with electricity, and an unbearable lightness swept my head and chest as though I had cooked off all my worries with drugs or alcohol. Ethel is the only woman who has ever made me feel this and I cannot explain it any other way except that she is mine and I am hers, and brother you know it when you find it.

"Hi uh, Ethel. Harry."

I was surprised to see Dane Harris behind us. I couldn't imagine him freely coming to a social event.

"Well hi there, Dane. Millie here?"

"Ah, no Ethel."

"Dane, good to see you."

"Harry, ah...do you have a minute?"

No. "Sure."

"I need to talk to you. Ah, more or less man to man."

"I'll be right back, Ethel. I'll get us a couple sandwiches."

"Don't be long."

I followed him away from the crowd, off toward the hillside bleachers against the concession stand on the edge of the football field where it lay like a quarry or a dry lakebed below the school.

"What's up, Dane?"

"I don't, I don't know. I got...I don't know."

"Okay, calm down. I think we were all sort of sideways the other night."

"How do you do it?"

"Do what? Screw up all the time and not get hit by a truck?"

But Dane didn't laugh.

"Millie and I, we're not...it isn't..."

I waited while he took a deep breath.

"You and Ethel seem to have it all figured out."

I laughed. "No, I think we're figuring it out as we go."

"Me too."

The look of sadness that washed over him made my stomach turn over.

"What's wrong, Dane?"

His face colored and he seemed scarcely able to catch his breath.

"It isn't...I-I think...never mind, Harry. Thanks." He slapped me on the shoulder and walked off, then seemed to realize he wasn't going anywhere useful and changed directions.

"That's an odd damn feller," Jay Powell said, appearing at my elbow.

"Yup."

"You talked to Vee Clare yet?"

"Nope."

"Well you about to, come with me."

But I was still thinking about Dane Harris. People kept approaching me as though I had any ability to help them. Most days I felt lucky if I handled my own affairs with any aplomb, and any thought of helping others seemed a burden far beyond the limited scope of my abilities.

CHAPTER SIX

IT WAS STILL quite warm the night Dane Harris died. Freda came by and told Ethel, and they called on Millie to see how she was holding up and offer what assistance they could.

It had been an eventful couple of weeks. My Ford was totaled; but Veola Clare had hired me on to stock shelves at the Circle Market, and I found the work pleasant enough, if repetitive. It was hard on my knees and my feet were terrible at the end of the day, but it was also good exercise and I felt in my best shape since the Army.

Mr. Clare had sent me to see his brother Conor about a car, and he gave me a deal on a Pontiac Bonneville. It was a couple years old but had never been owned, and he came down on the price until I didn't feel justified in saying no. It had a lot of chrome and funny tailfins, and the paint was an oceanic color that recalled the odor of saltwater and put me in mind of my old Hudson.

Saturday we went to the funeral and hugged Millie and reassured her that she was surrounded by people who cared. Frank was even there. He was freshly shaven and barbered, but the sportcoat and trousers, fit for his former frame, gave him the appearance of an overdressed scarecrow. Ignoring me and Ethel, he quietly slipped out after the service and did not attend the reception.

Tuesday I had the day off from work and went out to John's to get the mail. Among the usual assortment of bills and letters from Ethel's relatives, was a letter addressed to me from Mildred Harris, offering me a job. Ethel was at the sink when I came home, scrubbing the last yield of squash from our garden for the season. When she'd dried her hands on a dishtowel, looked over the carefully folded bit of note paper and handed it back, she studied me briefly and picked up her vegetable brush.

"Well if y'don't want to do it, don't."

"She's not thinking clearly. I'm a stock boy, not a detective."

"Hieronymus Cogbill you are many things, and stock boy is the least of 'em."

At least she was back in my corner.

"At any rate, Mildred has questions and she thought you might help. We ought to let her know one way or t'other, so you'll have to make up your mind."

Later, after we cleaned up the squash and ate lunch and did some other things, I got in my sea-hued Pontiac and went back to the store in Gera to use the phone. Mildred Harris was glad I called and said she was home and I could stop by anytime that afternoon. I bought a newspaper and an RC Cola from John because I felt guilty.

I drove out to Purkins' Corner and west on Route 3, through King George Courthouse and Arnold's Corner, then north on Comorn Road, a small two-lane headed towards route 218 at Osso. Osso was an old two-story house with a tin roof, a decorative front-facing gable, and a wide porch with ornate posts and railings, on the southeast corner of the T intersection. A few miles further on 218 was a more modern home, a small bungalow-type house with an umbrella clothesline in the yard and a white '59 Galaxie in the driveway.

I parked behind the Galaxie and stepped up on the porch. I tried tapping on the stormdoor at first, then tentatively opened it and used a small brass knocker in the middle of the door. I heard Mildred holler "just a minute" and then there was a shuffling from inside and a clank, and the door sucked open and Mildred stood there in her cat's eye glasses and pea green dress, her dark hair piled high on top of her head.

"Oh, Harry, you made it. Come on in."

Her living room was full of flower arrangements people had given her, and cards, and I felt momentarily ill-prepared as I'd brought her nothing. But I remembered then that Ethel had already done for us. Millie led me into the kitchen, asking if she could get me anything to drink.

"Just coffee, if you have any."

In the hallway just before the kitchen, I noticed the framed photo of Millie and Dane on their wedding day. He had apparently always been an awkward-looking man, bald and narrow-faced, with a black fringe and tortoise-shell frames; even on his wedding day his smile somehow looked forced.

"How are you and Ethel getting on?" Millie asked, as I lurked uncomfortably between the Frigidaire and the formica table. "And sit down, for goodness sakes, you're making me nervous!"

The chairs were formed of chrome tubing and vinyl padding, and the table's legs were chrome too, as were the edges of the formica top, which was printed with little pink and blue boomerangs. There was a rotating spice rack backed up against the wall, and a napkin holder and a little sugar bowl with a lid and a notch for the spoon.

"We're good," I said. "Although I wonder why she puts up with me."

The percolator sighed and farted rhythmically. She had a fancier one than mine, electric, white with blue cornflowers stenciled on the side and a black plastic stand under it.

She laid out a small plate of cookies, poured us each a cup and sat down across from me.

"How about you, Millie? I was sorry to hear about Dane."

"Thank you," she said, "for agreeing to help me out."

"Always, but I have to warn you, I'm not much of a detective, whatever Ethel may have told you."

"Stop doing that," Millie said.

"Excuse me?"

"Stop putting yourself down."

"But I'm really not a detective," I said. "though I occasionally detect."

"That isn't the point, Hieronymus. Do you respect your wife?"

"You know I do."

"Then respect the fact that she sees your worth. Even if you don't."

I sensed I had touched a nerve. I've always been bad at people.

"You're right, Millie. I'm sorry. What is it I can do for you?"

"It's about the circumstances of Dane's passing."

"I didn't know there was anything unusual."

"Well, Sheriff Powell ruled out foul play, and the doctors did say it was a heart attack, but I just can't help thinking..."

I didn't prod her. I didn't really know what to say, or what to ask, and it was hard to imagine what she was getting at. She'd come home from helping her sister with a new baby out in Culpeper, to find Dane laying across the bed in his boxers and undershirt. His pants were folded over a chair and the closet door was open. There was nothing too peculiar about any of it, except that Dane's heart had stopped.

"Well he was on the wrong side of the bed," Millie said. "And I've never seen him put his pants over the chair like that, and why do that with the closet door open, that's where he usually put them. The hanger wasn't even out. And...Hieronymus you mustn't tell anyone, but there were two glasses in the sink, and I just have a bad feeling, and I'm so embarrassed..." she choked up a little and I took her hand.

"It's probably nothing, Mill."

And I figured that was probably the truth. Dane wasn't the type, and I said so. I'd seen the man put a half-eaten sandwich in his pants pocket, for God's sake. I didn't mention that part.

"There wasn't lipstick on one of the glasses or anything?"

"No, nothing like that."

"Well there you go, they were probably both his, or one of his friends stopped by. I don't want to take your money on this, Mildred, it isn't worth it."

"Now damn it, you will take my money and you will do this for me, and that's all there is to it."

"I don't feel good about this, Millie."

"It would put my mind at ease."

Assuming I was right about Dane, sure. I exhaled.

"If you're sure this is what you want."

She said it was, and she gave me an advance, which I tried like hell to refuse. I even tried to forget it when I left, but she caught me and pressed it back into my hand. The only thing more embarrassing than receiving charity was taking money from a widow.

That evening Ethel and I went to dinner in a little red-brick restaurant on the southbound side of 301, a little ways south of the circle. King George County's first pizzeria didn't look like much from the outside, just sort of a house with a couple plate glass windows and a swinging door with a cowbell. There were flyers taped to the windows advertising a sort of beauty pageant the pizzeria was sponsoring. Some lucky young lady would be crowned the Pizza Queen. I thought it sounded a bit tasteless, but it didn't seem like any business of mine.

Inside the tables were covered in red-checked linens, and Roy Orbison's melancholy tremolo issued from a jukebox. There was a Pizza Queen flyer on every table. We drank Cokes and split a pie with pepperoni, sausage, black olives and green peppers. I could live without the plant matter, but Ethel was equally unenthusiastic about my selection of savory meats, so as always we met each other halfway.

"I'm sure if we ask they'll make it half and half."

"You take the good with the bad," she said.

The place was enjoying a brisk business, but it was still new and pizza a novelty in our little slice of rural Virginia. The owners, Fred and Ernest Vittorio, were young brothers fresh out of the Navy. The warm smells of rising dough, hot tomato sauce and spiced meats dripping with grease filled whatever airspace Orbison's voice hadn't staked its claim to.

"So you took Millie's case?"

"It's not a case. I'm not a detective. She's just worried Dane might've been messing around on her."

"Not Dane."

"I know, he was a fish out of water in any social situation."

"He was a fish up a tree."

"It's a waste of her money."

"Not if it puts her mind at ease."

"I know."

"Still thinking about that William fella?"

"The guy I worked with wouldn't have done what they say he did."

"You cain't save everybody."

"I hadn't saved anybody, Ethel. When we met you asked for my help. What did I accomplish? I mean really?"

"Well you got yourself a pretty damned fine wife, for starters."

I couldn't argue with that.

"I did. But I didn't finish what I started, for you and your family."

"You cain't change Uncle Jack's mind."

"I'm just worried this thing is spreading like a cancer in the county."

"Hieronymus, we got a county full of old bootleggers and the children and grandchildren of Confederate spies. People around here don't get up in each other's business. The government interferes enough already. Nobody wants to know what the neighbors are into. The worst thing would be to lose respect."

I wondered if it wouldn't be worse to sleep on corruption, to let it fester in the dark, and wake one day to find the sun shining on nothing but gangrenous ruin. After we ate, paid the tab, and left a healthy tip for our harried young waitress, Carol, we crunched across the gravel lot. Halfway to the car I noticed a familiar Lincoln Continental parked around the side of the building. It hadn't been there when we arrived, and I hadn't seen Adagio come in the front door, which must have meant he was familiar enough to come in the back.

"Why is it that guy keeps turning up?"

"Please be careful, Cogbill."

Wednesday after work I stopped by the store in Gera and used John's phone. I dialed a Massachusetts number and waited for the nasal voice with the pancaked vowels to come on the line.

"Mahoney, Robbery-Homicide."

"Hello, Len."

"Who is this?"

"Harry."

"Cogbill? Been a while. Congrats on your wedding, by the way. You get the card I sent?"

"It was a sympathy card."

"That is true."

"You addressed it to my wife."

"It was heartfelt. What do you want?"

"I need a favor."

"Do they not have police in Virginia?"

"They don't like me."

"Christ, I don't like you. I gotta start screening my calls."

"Remember last year, you looked up those Greek mafia guys for me?"

"Sure, how can I forget? The homicide rate in Boston is so low I just stick my thumb up my keister and wait for you to call."

"There was an attorney, out of Brooklyn, named Hector Adagio. You didn't have anything on him."

"Okay, that half rings a bell. So what?"

"Turns out he's licensed in Kansas City, Palm Beach and L.A., too."

Silence on the other end.

"Len?"

"I'm thinking."

"Is there any chance...?"

"Is that guy actually there in Mayberry or wherever the Christ you live?"

"Yeah."

"Tread lightly, Cogbill."

The tone in his voice was sober.

"Is there something I should know?"

"Maybe. Those cities you named. Brooklyn, Palm Beach, Kansas City and L.A. That combination mean anything to you?"

It did, but I wanted to hear him say it. "Should it?"

"They're Gambino territories. Remember your boy Lazos? One of theirs. Do not step on this guy's nuts."

"He keeps stepping on mine."

"What did you do?"

"Nothing. Well. Shit."

"Cogbill..."

"There was this busboy at my old job. Little Italian guy, New York. Bum leg. One day Adagio walks in and scares the life right out of him."

"How's that involve you?"

"The guy with the leg, Joey, thinks he's my friend. Now Adagio thinks so too. He knows where I live, he's been to the house."

"Hang up and call the Feds."

"I don't want to involve the government."

"Don't get all Rothbardian or Randian or whatever, okay? Just do it."

"I want to know who Joey really is. Adagio called him Tony."

"Well that narrows it down to about a hundred-thousand Italians in New York."

"He limps."

"I'll make some calls. Just do me a favor and call the Feds, okay? And make sure your wife's got that shotgun loaded."

CHAPTER SEVEN

JAY POWELL was on his way out of the office when I caught up with him. His octagonal hat was perched on his head at a jaunty angle, and he was buttoning the waist-length jacket over his blocky middle when he looked up and saw me.

"Cogbill. Unless you're inviting me to dinner I ain't got time."

"It's about Hector Adagio."

"Who?"

I took Adagio's card out of my pocket and handed it to him.

"The guy who spooked my coworker back at Horne's."

"Willy Johnson?"

"Not him, the one that ran me off the road."

"You think he did it on purpose?"

"No, I think he's scared. Adagio's got offices in New York, Palm Beach, Kansas City and L.A. You know what that means, Sheriff?"

"He's a bigshot."

"Those are Gambino cities, Jay."

"Oh now come on, Cogbill, why you always looking for mob guys down here? You think one of them boys is running chickens? Smuggling eggs across state lines? Where's the crime?"

"You know why organized crime exists, sheriff?"

"Because people don't like bein' told what to do, mainly."

"Because regulation doesn't determine the market. Because people want what they want and need what they need and will do what they have to do to get it."

"Well God damn it, idn't that what I just said?"

"What do you know about Fred and Ernest Vittorio?"

"Cogbill who d'you think you are? In the first place this idn't an interrogation, and in the second if it was, you on the wrong side of the badge."

"Adagio's car was parked around the side of their restaurant. It wasn't there when we went in. We never saw him. He went in the back door, Sheriff."

"No shit? Let's go back in the office, call J. Edgar Hoover."

"This is why I don't invite you to parties."

"I done told you before. You don't have a crime to report, it ain't much I can do. My job is to keep my people out of trouble. That includes you."

"God forbid the sheriff should care about criminals in the county."

"Now Hieronymus I'm fit to knock you out and mail you back to your wife. Just do your job and let me do mine."

"Right. Forget it."

"Don't make a widow out of her, will you? Why truck with other people's bidness? 'Specially if they might be gangsters."

He got out a lighter and set fire to Adagio's card, dropped it in a pedestal ashtray in the hall.

"Go home, Cogbill."

I watched his broad back disappear into the blue evening light.

The next day I was putting price stickers on barrel-shaped jars of pickles, and lining them up on a shelf in the Circle Market.

The lids on the jars said "MOUNT ROSE BRAND PICKLES," and underneath that in smaller letters, "PACKERS AND GROWERS MOUNT ROSE CANNING CO. KING GEORGE, VA." It was blue and white and had a picture of snow-capped mountains, although there are no mountains near King George.

My boss, Vee Clare, came over to give me a hand. He was a big guy with dark hair, glasses and a high forehead.

I said, "I used to make these."

"You worked at the Pickle Factory?"

"My supervisor and I didn't get along."

"You seem like a educated man, Cogbill. There a reason you don't set your sights a little higher?"

"I just want Ethel to be proud of me. Sometimes I'm not sure why she puts up with me."

"I used to work for a nice Jewish family up DC," Clare said. "Taught me everything I know about business. Eventually I got it in my head to marry their daughter."

"Did you?"

"Aw hell, it was a joke to her. 'Why Vee, your salary wouldn't buy my nylons.' But look at me now."

"Looks like you're doing pretty good."

"The point being there's two kinds of women in this world: them that sees your worth and them that don't. If you want to know why your wife puts up with you, I'd say it's because she's the first kind."

"I guess I just never figured out what kind of career path fits me."

"Man's got to take a leap once in a while. What is it gets you out of bed in the morning?"

"I don't reckon I've ever quite worked that out. I do a little sjde work as an investigator."

"Is that right? For Jay?"

"Not hardly. Just on an independent basis."

"Well now that's a hell of a leap."

"Do you know Tom Boone?"

Clare stopped his work and regarded me across the aisle.

"Not well. He lives out at Nanzatico."

"Yes he does. He's in real estate investment."

"Lot of that around here. Thing we got the most of, is land."

"As I've been reminded recently."

"What you investigating him for?"

"I'm not, really. He's a person of interest." I thought of Adagio's description of Joey DeLarosa.

"Well, Elwood Mason'll probably be by the Restaurant later. Boone's in real estate, Elwood'll've met him."

Mason was Clerk of the Court.

Since about 1946 Vee Clare had operated a supermarket and a restaurant at Edge Hill. When the state decided to widen 301, Clare was eminent domained out of both businesses and a good deal of other land he owned along the corridor, but the money he got from all of it was enough to replace both his store and his restaurant, in upgraded form, near their original locations.

The new Circle Family Restaurant was hip-roofed and weathervaned, resembling a HoJo, just north of the Circle Market. Inside was spacious and modern, brightly-lit, all curtained plate-glass windows and vinyl booths. Clare took me over and introduced me to Mason.

"You want supper or anything, Cogbill?" I believe Vee would even have paid for it, but I declined.

"I'll do for Ethel and myself when I get on home."

"Cup of coffee?"

"I never turn down coffee."

Mason looked at me over a cup of his own, chewing green beans and maybe some sort of thought pattern I could only guess at. He had a narrow jaw and a broad forehead, fair hair and a long, straight nose. His eyes were piercing beneath sharply peaked brows. I made him fortyish, give or take a couple years.

"Cogbill. Not Coghill?"

"No sir, I'm from Chesterfield." Coghill was a King George family, and this was a question I had grown accustomed to answering in the time I'd lived here.

"Maybe distantly related to the Coghills?"

"That is possible."

"Still, name's familiar to me."

"Can't imagine why."

"Vee said you had something I could help you with?"

"Maybe. I met Tom Boone a couple weeks ago."

"What'd you think of him?"

"Pretty much what I think of any venereal disease."

Mason polished off his beans, put the little bowl on the empty plate with its swirls of gravy and crumbs of beef. Regarded his coffee with a hawk-like intensity.

"Well, you definitely met him."

"What about you?"

"Guy has his hand in a lot of land deals, but around here who doesn't?"

"So I'm always being reminded."

"What's your interest in him?"

"You read the papers, Mr. Mason?"

"Sure."

"So you know the name William Johnson."

"Yep."

"Boone's his landlord."

"Okay."

"The guy William allegedly murdered was the builder on one of Boone's projects."

"George Siever, yeah. Cloverdale. You talked to any of Siever's employees?"

"Think it'll do any good?"

"Come by the office tomorrow, I'll give you a name and a number. You talked to Jay?"

"He damned sure has." Jay Powell put his jacket on a hook by the booth and slid in beside Mason.

"Sheriff."

"Howdy Jay."

"Vee, Elwood. Cogbill."

"Evening, Sheriff."

"I thought I told you to leave it alone."

"You say a lot of things, Jay. Sometimes it's hard to keep track."

The front door sucked open and a guy came in shivering without a jacket, his cheeks flushed and his mouth all puckered up in frustration. He was a big man with soft features; great sloping shoulders, thick pale arms that bulged with muscle under a coating of smooth, freckled fat.

"There a pizza place somewhere around here?" he asked the room at large.

Everything sort of stopped.

"We don't sell pizza," Clare said. "I can get you an open-faced roast beef, or—"

"You don't unnerstand, I'm meeting my cousin. At the pizza place, assuming this ice-cold bog hadn't swallowed it up. Uh, Ernest's or something?"

He had a heavy brow with prominent arches, but his nose was pinched and faintly porcine, and his face had the broad, flat, doughy look of an Irish farmer. There was one sparse eyebrow above his right eye, and only a few wayward hairs above the other. A toothpick protruded from between fat, pink lips. He wore a camp shirt and chinos, and a trilby with the snap-brim turned up in front. His left forearm was pink with sunburn, and his cheeks shone like apples.

"The Ernest Pie, you done overshot by a few miles," Powell said.

"Thanks Chief." His eyes glittered darkly; actually glittered isn't the right word because there seemed to be no light in them at all. They were a little too wide, the iris not touching either lid. If it wasn't for the eyes I might not have made him.

"How was the drive up from Florida?"

"How you know I'm from Florida?"

"Where else do they dress like that?"

"How 'bout you deep-six the attitude, wiseass?"

Possibly Navy. His workingman's hands and big dumb demeanor said enlisted, not Annapolis. Too big for submarines. A sailor wouldn't have much small-arms training, so if my estimation of the man was correct, he must've put some time in elsewhere learning the skills of his current trade. Maybe recreationally. Or maybe he'd been a cop or bondsman after he got his papers.

He bulled on back out to the parking lot and there was a pregnant moment before the dining sounds resumed. Mason looked me over with an appraising eye, as though he were raising his opinion of me by a notch or two. Clare grinned and patted my shoulder, and Jay gave me a sharp look.

"What was all that stuff about Florida?"

"I know a Guido when I see one. Even if he happens to be Irish. Ten to one his so-called cousin is Hector Adagio and the meeting's about a job. Maybe looking for Joey, or William. Maybe the sort of thing you ought to check on. Sheriff."

"It ain't that I don't care, you know that right? But I cain't go harassing citizens in their private bidness just cause you have a feeling."

"I was right last time, wasn't I?"

"You almost got Ethel Burkitt killed last time. Suppose you're right. Suppose Boone and Adagio somehow pushed the Johnson boy into killing that Siever fella. You want them kind of people knocking on your door?"

"They already are, Jay. That's the problem."

"They threatened you?"

"Not really."

"Good. Don't give 'em no reason to."

"Tell that to Joey DeLarosa. He broke in my house."

"Now damn it Cogbill, whyn't you tell me that to start with?"

"It wasn't clear to me that it would matter."

"Man like that come around my place making trouble, I'd kick his rear end all the way to Stafford," Clare said.

"I threw him out on his ass," I said.

"Well Cogbill, since you done reported an honest-to-Jesus crime for a change, I'll look into it."

"Thank you, Sheriff."

"You happen to know where he lives?"

"No."

"So I'll have to call Caroline County and get them to check with Horne's. Give me a few days."

"A few days? I could drive out there right now and—"

"But you won't. You hear me?"

Mason and Clare were looking expectantly in my direction.

"Yes Sheriff. I hear you."

"You fellers heard him, right? You heard that."

Mason grinned, and Clare's shoulders moved in silent laughter. I put down a quarter for the coffee and Clare pushed it back to me. I thanked him for the coffee, Mason for the talk, and Jay for promising to look at Joey. Then I walked back across the lot.

Friday after work I swung by the courthouse. Under the columned portico was a set of white-painted doors with a fanlight set in red brick. Inside was a small open area with a wooden bench, a water fountain, and a taxidermied eagle in a glass box. Directly ahead were the doors for the single courtroom. A narrow yellow hall ran laterally through the building, and to the right it led to a vault door with a step up into Mason's domain. There was a counter inside the door, and large banks of heavy, bound volumes containing court records and land deeds going back to the founding of King George County in 1720.

It was said that George Washington's father, Augustine, had filed his Will at King George Courthouse – although that building, somewhere near Canning on the Rappahannock, was long gone, its bricks occasionally surfacing in the mud whenever farmers turned the soil for planting. During the Civil War, the

Yankees had a reputation for burning court records and so the Clerk at that time, William Brown, hid as many of the records as he could in the attic at his home, Waverley.

Behind the counter in the vault was Mason's lair, an office partially enclosed with glass. All the exterior windows in the vault were barred. Mason's chair sat empty behind his desk, and an assistant, filing some papers, looked me over.

"Can I help you?"

"Yes, I was looking for Mr. Mason."

She nodded her head at a point over my shoulder. I turned around to see Elwood coming in, some papers and a couple of books under his left arm. He stuck his right hand out, and we shook.

"Mr. Cogbill-not-Coghill, glad you could make it. Step into my office."

He closed the door behind us and put his papers on the desk.

"I don't reckon Jay knows you're here." He sat down in his chair and waved me to one across from him, and grinned suddenly. "Better forgiveness than permission, right?"

"Lately."

"Jay's a good man, Mr. Cogbill. He wants you to be safe. It's his job."

"It is."

"People like the idea that we live in a sleepy little place with palm-fans on front porches and gossip at the post office. They don't want to know about the other stuff."

"Bootleggers and rebel spies?"

"For a start."

He took a small slip of paper from the pocket of his blazer and pushed it across the desk to me. It said Vernon Grigsby in a looping hand, the E like a backward 3. It had an address and a telephone number with it.

"He knew Siever. He'll speak plain."

"Friends?"

"No. Not at all."

"Mr. Mason, is it possible you could help me with one more thing?"

"That probably depends on the thing."

"The Ernest Pie. The Vittorios' place. Any chance I can see the property records there?"

"Of course. They're public. You have about five minutes, we can do it now."

I stood, tucked the paper in my pocket, and thanked Mason. He led me to the outer office, referenced a ledger, and took me straight to the book in question. He laid it out on the slanted surface on top of the file shelf it was in, and flipped through the pages until he found it. The Vittorios were leasing the building from a company based out of Jersey City. The President was Hector Adagio. The Secretary was Dimitrios Vasiliou. Jimmie the Greek.

"Get what you needed?"

"I think so."

When I stopped for the mail in Gera, John had a callback message for me from Len.

"Said he was urgent, he'd wait up at the office long as he could."

"Thanks, John." I rang Len back and he picked up almost immediately.

"Hi Len."

"Cogbill. Did you call the feds?"

"Len..."

"Goddammit, Cogbill, don't mess around with your wife's safety."

"What have you got, Len?"

"I think I got a line on your Joey DeLarosa. Your guy Adagio, he's in imports, right? Handles some discrete shipping concerns for the Family. That's Family with a capital F, you understand?"

"Drugs?"

"Nah, Carlo Gambino don't like drugs. Back in March, they were expecting a sensitive delivery. Somebody sold them out, rival gang shows up to intercept. It's a clusterfuck, sorry, I sound like one a them now. It was a mess, okay? My guy in New York said they were hosing blood off the dock all the next day. Thing is, one of the dock workers, he goes missing. Nobody knows if he's alive or dead, but they traced the leak to him. Name's Antonio DiRossi."

"Tony."

"The feds would really like to talk to him."

"I guess they would."

"I called them."

"Damn it, Len. I already got the local sheriff on it."

"Not for long. You'll thank me later."

The next morning I woke early, Ethel's head on my chest and one pale leg across my waist. The faint strawberry fragrance of her hair took me back to the day I first understood that I never wanted to be without her. I extricated myself from her sleeping embrace, put on pants and made my way to the kitchen. I got the percolator going while I cubed a couple of potatoes and diced a small yellow onion, and fried them up with a big hunk of butter and a sprinkling of Sauer's coarse ground black pepper.

Fawkes whined at me.

"Is that so?"

He whined again, and made one of those weird vulpine vocalizations that was somewhere between a bark and a wheeze.

"Oh," I said, "well that explains it."

He seemed to have a lot on his mind.

The potatoes took about fifteen minutes, so while that was going I opened a can of hash and scrambled some eggs. The smell brought Ethel out in a little while, wearing one of my shirts. She put Fawkes out in his pen, then said grace over our meal.

After breakfast I took a shower and, it being Saturday, headed out to begin interviews on the Dane Harris thing. Our driveway was a mile long out to Gera Road, and west on Gera led to Millbank and I turned right, going north until I came out between the school and St. Anthony's church, then turned right and joined Route 3 near Willow Hill, Vee Clare's house, just short of Arnold's Corner. At the corner I took a right onto route 206, passed the dirt driveway of Waverley on the left, and wound along the tree-lined way until I saw the Weedonville Post Office and made a right onto Eden Drive. Eden Estates was a new subdivision, still in progress, built to accommodate the influx of people coming to work at the Naval Weapons Laboratory in Dahlgren.

Maynard Carter was a mathematician. I'm not sure what he did as a civilian employee of the Navy, but I'm sure it paid pretty well and probably had to do with blowing stuff up, which seems like good work if you can get it. Two little boys were running around the yard with bath towels tucked into the neck of their t-

IN THE TRACKLESS WILD | 85

shirts, arms outstretched like George Reeves on television. The one was fussing to the other that Batman couldn't fly and he'd have to stay behind. The younger kid insisted Batman definitely could fly or he wouldn't have a cape. His brother wasn't buying it. There was a lot of crying.

"Hey mister, can Batman fly?"

"I don't think so. I think Captain Marvel could, he could do about anything Superman does."

"Captain who?"

"Uh, he was this kid who yelled 'Shazam!' and lightning hit him and he turned into a big Superman guy who looked like Fred MacMurray? Red suit? White cape?"

"Wow!" the kid yelled. "SHAZAM!" And he took off running after his brother.

My day was unlikely to get better from here, but I stepped up on the porch and rang the doorbell anyway. The house was a brick rancher with a small front stoop and brown shingles. It was so new the paint on the shutters was fresh and the mortar between the bricks looked clean and smooth. There was a Chevy Nomad and a Ford Falcon in the driveway.

The woman who answered the door looked tired, and a little frazzled, and she did not invite me in. Instead, when I asked after Mr. Carter, she summoned him and disappeared into the house.

"We're not interested in buying anything, mister."

Maynard's hair was a tangled mass that didn't look like it'd seen a comb in a week. His khakis fit him poorly, bagging off his ass and covering his slippers, and he had a short-sleeved button-down with a pen in the breast pocket and crumbs down the front. His cheeks were rosy and his smile was strangely dark. He had thin lips and his mouth was a little too wide for his face.

"Well I'm not selling anything, Mr. Carter. My name's Harry Cogbill, I'm working for Mildred Harris."

"Oh. Yeah, poor Dane."

"Poor Millie," I said.

"Yeah, true, I guess Dane isn't the one hurting."

"I hate to bring this up, but Millie's a little concerned that Dane might have been entertaining a guest when he died."

"What, like a friend?"

"Well, for example. Maybe a special friend."

"What, like a work friend?"

"Like a lady friend, Maynard."

"I never thought Dane was the type."

"Me neither. Still, what if he was? Can you think of anyone, maybe from work, that he might have been seeing? Did he have a secretary, or…?"

"No. I mean Christ, socializing? Who's got time for that? Let alone fraternizing. Dane?"

"He didn't talk to anybody?"

"I don't watch what people do. It's boring."

When I left Carter's place I drove out to meet Vern Grigsby. The address was out near Igo, west of Arnold's Corner and nearly to Stafford County, so when I left the fledgling Eden Estates I turned west on 206 and made a right onto Indiantown Road until its terminus on 218 at Ambar, the white, columned face of Mount Stuart on its knoll behind a gravel loop where I turned left toward Stafford. At a place called Mustoe I turned left again onto Lambs Creek Church Road.

Grigsby's house turned out to be a trailer in the woods. He was sitting on a folding beach chair drinking sun tea and shooting at tin cans he'd hung on strings from branches along the edge of the forest. He was wearing a strap undershirt and a pair of canvas trousers. He wasn't excited about company, but he didn't go inside and shut the door, either.

"Vern Grigsby?"

"Who's asking?"

"Thomas Jefferson, obviously."

"Oh great, a wiseass." He plinked a can.

"Do you mind not doing that?"

"If you're gonna come on my property and wise off, yeah, I mind."

"My name's Harry Cogbill. I just had a couple questions about George Siever."

"He's dead."

"No kidding."

"Was some black what did it."

"Allegedly," I said.

"Hey, I ain't all broke up about it. Siever couldn't pour piss out a boot if the instructions was printed on the heel."

"Not a mental giant, then?"

"You know what he was doing?"

"Building houses?"

"Yeah and them boys in Boston spilt some tea. I wouldn't call them things houses, on account of I wouldn't call what he had us doing, building."

"Come again?"

"He won the bid by lowballing the investment group on the prices, right? Only the price he quoted was a crock."

"He couldn't do it?"

"Christ himself couldn't do it, and you know he was a carpenter."

"Among other things."

"The floor joists are spaced twice as far as they ought to be, the ceilings too. He used hospital windows."

"Hospital windows?"

"Yeah, the kind that you can't just open and jump out. He got a good deal on a load of 'em."

"The houses are junk?"

"They're a disaster. They look okay now. In twenty or thirty years? I'd rather be living in this dump."

Lamb's Creek Church, which gave the road its name, was built in 1767 and was a single-story red brick building with a hipped roof and no steeple, and like most things in King George it sat hunched among craggy trees in a depression that would turn to bog in a hard rain. It had been desecrated during the Civil War, used for stables by the Union Army. The road, a narrow byway, ended at Route 3 near Lamb's Creek itself, and as I drove back East toward King George Courthouse, a huge brick house called Rokeby sat on its hill like a fortress overlooking the countryside at the far end of a long driveway with a gate. The house had been Burnside's headquarters during the Fredericksburg Campaign.

I found Sheriff Powell in Tommy's Snack Bar.

"Siever was stretching out materials to come in under bid."

"Well what the hell I'm supposed to do, dig him up and arrest him?"

"Boone and Adagio had him killed. Come on, it's obvious."

"Sit down, have some coffee. You're making a scene."

I sat down.

"Now what did I tell you about detectin' without a license?"

"You're letting William take the fall."

"There are witnesses, Cogbill."

"There may also have been duress."

"That dudn't make him not guilty."

"It doesn't make Boone and Adagio not guilty either."

"Harry. I got to tell you something you ain't gonna like, so you got to promise to keep your cool. You hear me?"

"Yes Jay. I hear you."

My stomach and temples tightened in anticipation.

"I called Caroline County about your boy DeLarosa."

"He was involved in a mob shootout in New York."

"Shut your mouth. I don't want to hear it. I'm telling you I got shut down."

"Shut down?"

"You heard me."

"What, by the Feds?"

"Look, forget the star for a minute okay? I'm talking to you as a friend. You got to let this mess alone."

CHAPTER EIGHT

THE WEATHER had turned cold and the sun had begun its annual retreat to the throne of judgment from which it cast its pale, solitary eye upon the grey and barren earth. Smoke issued from chimney pipes like the breath of dragons asleep upon their hoarded treasure. The engine of my Pontiac sounded as feeble as my spirits as it conveyed me, wheezing, to the Circle Market in the mornings.

It was Wednesday and dawn came sleepy and dull, the humped forms of ash, white oak and sweet gum spectral silver beneath the orange creamsicle sky. I had the day off, so after breakfast I put on my mackinaw and fedora and kissed Ethel goodbye, and went out to find Joey. Dry, hot air issued from the vents at my feet. At a filling station on route 17 just west of Port Royal, I thumbed through the directory under a payphone hoping I'd get lucky, but there were no DeLarosas. So instead I called Horne's. I was maybe a quarter mile away, and I could see the yellow roof and the red oval sign and the shimmering cars at the gas pumps, or parked nose-in toward the gleaming plate-glass windows like hogs at a trough.

The hostess who answered the phone at the counter asked me to hold a moment. Her name was Rose, and she was maybe twenty. She worked part-time to help her parents cover the mortgage on their home. I could hear the sound of the breakfast crowd as she directed someone to sit where they'd like before she asked me how she could help.

I tried my best impression of Len Mahoney.

"Yeah this is Fred MacMurray, no relation. I'm with a collections agency and I need to speak to Joey DeLarosa about delinquent payments on a '53 Chevrolet."

"He don't work here no more."

"Well now that is unfortunate. He's a difficult fellow to track down. I wonder if I have the correct address for him, would you mind seeing what you have on file?"

"I don't think management would like that."

I didn't feel any pride over what I was about to do.

"Yeah, I get it. It's just my boss is pretty cross with me and the bank is starting to make noise about the money they lent this DeLarosa guy, and if I don't find him I'm liable to be out on my keister. My wife's pinching pennies as it is, we got a baby on the way. Look I'm sorry I dumped all that on you."

"Don't sweat it. Let me see what I can do."

I clamped the payphone receiver between my shoulder and my ear, cupped a hand over the mouthpiece, and listened to the dull thrum of diner noise while an old guy who had a face like a sheaf of dried tobacco climbed down from the cab of a two-tone Chevy 3100. He wore denim overalls and a straw hat, and stuffed a wad of snuff in his cheek as he filled a big orange gas can from a pump under the port cochere. He had knuckles like the branches of an ancient oak tree.

In a few minutes Rose came back on and gave me an address near Skinker's Corner. I knew the road but not the address; there wasn't much out there. I'd have to stop at the nearest filling station or general store and hope the guy knew the place. I thanked Rose and hung up. The guy with the pickup looked straight at me and spat a stream of tobacco juice in the dirt.

"Morning."

"How many days 'til Spring?"

He grinned and chewed. "Must ain't got no kids."

"No sir."

"You lost?"

"N...well, kind of. You know Skinker's Corner?"

Ethel had fed Fawkes and was just sitting down with a cup of coffee and a book by James Michener when she heard a car in the driveway. It was Mildred Harris's Ford Galaxie, and she seemed uncomfortable as she stood on the porch.

"Well, Millie! Come on in. Can I get you coffee?"

"That's okay, thank you."

It was unclear to Ethel if that meant yes or no, so she got another cup and poured it full from my old tin percolator. She knew Millie liked cream and sugar, so she provided some, and they sat together in the living room while Fawkes snuffled around Mildred's feet and brought his twitching nose up onto the coffee table.

"Now Guy you know you don't like coffee. Last thing I need is a caffeinated fox climbing the drapes. What brings you out, Millie?"

There was a long, awkward silence. Ethel waited it out.

"I...it just isn't easy to say, Ethel. You have got to tell that man to leave me alone."

Ethel's mind filled with scenarios that she could make no sense of at all.

"What man?"

"Your father. He simply must stop calling on me."

Frank had put on aftershave and a clean shirt, and combed some cheap pomade into his steel grey hair. He sat in the

Studebaker in Millie's driveway with the motor running, regarding his leathered hands on the steering wheel, noting that he had forgotten to pick the dirt from beneath his nails. In any case it did not matter; the contour map of his fingerprints was etched in black soil and nicotine, and had been since he could remember.

He threw the transmission into reverse as he had every time he came here, but this time Millie came out to the car.

"Franklin Burkitt, I will call the sheriff if you don't tell me what on earth you're doing here."

He looked at her a little while, maybe a little too long, opening and closing dry lips. The truth being he wasn't sure himself.

"They left us," he said finally. "Your Dane and my Alice. They left us and it idn't fair."

"No it isn't."

"Ride with me to the store."

"Why?"

"Because I do everything alone. Ethel married that Cogbill loser, Christ knows why. Her mother was beautiful. I knowed her from the store. First time I seen her I had to have her. I couldn't imagine life without her. Then she was gone and it wadn't nothing I could do. I couldn't let Ethel see me cry. It would be too hard on her."

"I don't think that's true, Mr. Burkitt. I think it would have helped."

Ethel had told him something similar once, before she left. He didn't figure there was much sense to female thought, but Alice might have put him straight if she hadn't gone and died. Where was the sense in cancer, in leaving behind the people who needed you, whose world was cold and dark and full of only ash without your laughter?

All in a rush he felt the empty volume of time and space that had passed him by since anyone had laughed in his home. It wasn't even really a home anymore. It was just the place he toiled and sweated and drank away his anger and his bitterness.

His face was unaccountably damp. He punched the steering wheel and the horn bleated like a ewe birthing her lamb. He punched it again, and again, and choked on the taste of his impotence. The horn button broke off the wheel and he threw it across her lawn.

"You got to be lonely as me, Mildred. Ride with me. I don't know how to do this no more."

"I think you ought to go, Mr. Burkitt."

Her waist was a little too thick, her shoulders too round, her chin too much involved with her neck. But she was a woman, and he was a man; and although he couldn't quite fit them together in his mind, it had been some time since anything really fit to begin with.

"We could get married. It'd solve us both. I ain't so old it done unmanned me. You idn't too bad-looking. I'm a worker. You wouldn't want for nothing."

"Goodbye, Mr. Burkitt. I'll be calling Jay Powell directly."

I turned right onto a narrow way off 17, past a side entrance to AP Hill, deep among the copper, bronze, and ruby of the autumn forest, the craggy branches steepling over the gently undulating ribbon of narrow blacktop, until I found the copse of junipers and the dirty ruts of an unmarked drive the old man had described. The huge, forked, banana-colored leaf of a poplar plastered to my windshield. Apple-colored maple, cinnamon oak.

A small cabin slouched forlorn in a clearing like an overburdened pack mule. No smoke rose from the chimney and no green scarab of a Chevy sulked in its shadow. I had a feeling I recognized from my time in Europe; unarmed, I got the tire iron out of the trunk and put it in my coat. I looked around the clearing but saw no activity, no sign of life except for the crow I could hear somewhere in the treetops. I climbed three sloping steps and knocked on a heavy plank door. No sound of movement from within.

After a minute I gave up and circled around the house. It was dark inside and I could see nothing through the windows. In back there was a rusty grill under a dirty tarp, a lawnmower that had more grass on it than the yard, and a steel trash can that had been upended and rooted through by wild animals. There were chicken bones and grapefruit rinds all across the dusty lawn. Scraps of paper and cellophane mingled with the leaves.

The back door was open. The jamb was broken where the tongue of the lock was supposed to nest. Part of the trim around the door had fallen to the floor of the small galley kitchen. The lightswitch had no effect and there was no sound from any appliances. I guessed the power had been off a while. Leaves had blown in. There was a millipede in the sink. Baby skinks scattered across the floor like drops of liquid mercury, disappearing into crevices in the tile and under rustic cabinets. There was a smell of rotten meat, and I feared the worst. The master bedroom was empty, the bed unmade. Joey's clothes still in the closet. The second bedroom, with two single beds, both just bare mattresses. Nothing in the closet or dresser. Toothpaste and mouthwash in the bathroom, and a single frayed, speckled brush. White spots on the mirror.

The toilet seat was up. There was a toothpick floating in the bowl. I lifted the top off the tank but there was nothing inside, no plastic bags full of money or firearms. A house centipede looking like a creature from a cheap sci-fi matinee zipped around the bathtub. The smell was weaker here, and I made my way back to the kitchen. It was the food in the icebox: withered fruit webbed with white mold, a lettuce wrapper full of dirty sludge, and a package of greenish hamburger.

He'd sent his family away and stayed behind, at least for a while. Wherever Joey finally went, he'd packed light, and left unexpectedly. And I wasn't the first person who'd come looking for him. The feeling I'd had since I parked the car intensified. I took the lug wrench out of my coat and held it loosely in my right hand as I stepped out the back door. There were one-and-a-half Jack Webbs in the backyard.

"Stan. Ollie."

"Mr. Cogbill."

"You want to put the iron away, or you'd rather I shoot you?" Special Agent Clement Cathy was the full Webb. He wore no overcoat despite the chill, and his necktie had worked itself loose from the clip on his shirt-front and was flapping across his chest. His pistol was out but not pointed at me. He didn't identify himself as FBI but even if I didn't already know him, he wouldn't have to.

I dropped the lug wrench in the leaves.

"He didn't say to drop it."

"Well Agent Douglas, my car's out front and I didn't want to go reaching into my coat."

Douglas picked up the wrench and took me by the elbow.

"Let's go to your car, then."

Douglas was both younger and thinner than his partner. He was wearing Ray-Ban sunglasses and a short black trench coat with the belt flapping loose.

"I didn't do anything."

"We know. Your friend in Boston called the Bureau."

"And you chased a couple county sheriffs off a B&E investigation. Joey's one of your assets?"

We got to my car and Douglas popped the trunk. He poked around and dropped the lug wrench inside. Their plain black Ford was blocking the drive.

"Wait. You were watching the place. You know I didn't do anything because you know somebody already broke in. You should look at a man named Tom Boone. Also Hector Adagio, maybe Fred and Ernest Vittorio in King George. I think there's a button man up from Florida, big Irishman. A vet, possibly Navy."

Douglas was looking away, studying the treeline, and Cathy worked his wide black shoe in the grass like he'd stepped in dogshit.

"There's a lot going on you don't know about."

"The hell's that mean?"

"It means you should run on home to your wife and your pet fox and stock some shelves for Mr. Clare."

"Right," I said. "You know I find it really comforting how familiar you are with my personal business."

"We're on your side."

"Sure thing, Ollie. Thank you for your service."

That afternoon I melted some butter in a big Dutch oven, sautéed onion and garlic, and diced up a big russet potato. I had corn and lima beans from our garden that we'd blanched and frozen, and some of our tomatoes from the summer that Ethel had preserved in mason jars. I added these and chicken stock to the pot, and when it really started boiling I covered it and turned the stove down to let it simmer.

I put Fawkes out in his pen where he wouldn't bother the food, then went out to get some firewood from the pile beside the fence. I could smell the autumn scent of decay, not of flesh but of soft wood and rotting leaves, and the first crispness of frigid air.

I had no idea where Ethel had gone but I felt certain she'd be back before long, so I dragged a bundle of split logs inside and built up a fire in the hearth. When I checked the big pot on the stove, the corn and beans were tender, so I dumped in my leftover barbecue sauce, added Worcestershire and a package of leftover pulled pork I'd frozen several weeks ago and had brought down to thaw the night before. I kept the pot simmering, and then started preheating the oven.

While the oven ticked up I put some flour in a mixing bowl with a little baking powder, sugar, and salt, grated some butter into the mixture, and worked it together pretty well. Then I spread out some wax paper, floured it liberally, and folded the dough a while with my hands. When I was satisfied, I patted it out flat, and cut four or five biscuits out of the sheet of dough using a drinking glass. I placed them on a cookie sheet, reconstituted the trimmings, knocked out a couple more, and put them in the oven to bake.

I let Fawkes back in while I cleaned up the kitchen, and I found myself anticipating Ethel's delight at the aromas, although it has been my observation that the more expectation we attach to these moments the more apt they are to disappoint us. No matter how often I have these thoughts I am habitually unable to heed them.

While I was making Brunswick Stew and biscuits, Ethel was confronting her daddy about his recent behavior toward her friends. The red F-1 she drove seemed to carry her down the long orange wheel ruts to the old farmhouse of its own accord, the autumn sun descending in pale beams through billowing periwinkle clouds, the Aermotor choked with woody tendrils of grapevine, the tin roof of the house streaked with rust, the front porch step rotten and crumbling.

Stepping out of the truck she heard a commotion in the chicken coop, and found her father on the back step with a bloody hand, pulling fistfuls of feathers off a rooster with a broken neck.

"Son of a bitch got too high an opinion of himself," he said by way of explanation.

"You gonna cook that?"

"Confess I did give some thought to leaving it for the buzzards. Like as not I'll just burn it all to hell."

"Daddy do you know why I'm here?"

"Ain't see no suitcase."

"Millie Harris stopped by today."

"Christ."

"You need to leave my friends alone."

"Thought you wanted me to find somebody."

"Somebody appropriate, daddy. Somebody who wants to be found."

"Don't lecture me about age-appropriate relationships, babygirl. Dirty bastard you married's near old enough to be your daddy hisself."

"Well he didn't have to twist my arm. You get that it ain't the same, right?"

"He shot a kid."

The words were just noise at first, like someone speaking a language she did not know. Belatedly they assembled themselves in her mind, and even then she almost couldn't contextualize them.

"What? Who shot a kid?"

"Cogbill. It was in them papers they give me last year."

"You know that was gangsters trying to screw with us, right? You cain't believe anything they told you."

"So ask him yourself. You ain't safe. I just hope you figure it out before you get hurt."

The anger rose in her like an electric current from her toes and ignited something in her chest; her face colored and her hands balled up into fists and a lifetime of repressed anger exploded out of her like grapeshot, her voice rising in volume and intensity until she felt she was bellowing loud enough for the neighbors to hear half a mile away.

"Franklin Davis Burkitt, I knew you for a hard man and a fighter and an emotional coward, but I didn't never see you for the kind to sabotage your own daughter's happiness. You are a spiteful, hateful, selfish little pissant, and I don't care if you lock yourself in this shipwreck you call a house and burn it to the ground!"

As her voice rose his eyes fell, and his head, until he almost seemed to have fallen asleep; at last she saw that he was crying as he cradled the dead rooster in his arms. She thought briefly that the two of them, man and fowl, were nearly indistinguishable.

"I can't do it no more," he said.

"Well neither can I."

"Please."

"Don't call on Millie again."

"Please forgive me."

She left him sitting there as she rounded the house, climbed back in the truck, and drove way. As she pulled through the loop in front of the house she kept her eyes straight ahead and did not look for him to come after her.

I heard her come in the door as I was setting the table.

"Hey, welcome back. Was beginning to think I'd started supper too soon."

"Do I have a husband or a wife? Sometimes I cain't tell."

"Ouch."

"It smells good, Hieronymus, but I'm afraid I ain't too hungry."

"I thought..."

"Thought what? What did you do now? I know you didn't go to all this trouble for me if you ain't trying to atone for some damn thing."

"What? No, I just..."

"Well that's what this is all about, right? Get my pants off? Here. Here."

She stood half-undressed in the living room; it did not feel invitational although I admit that even in her anger, she has always turned me on.

"Ethel what the hell?"

"Sure, when you need it I got to drop everything and put the pieces back together, but when it's me all you can do is stand there and look at me like a lost child. Well don't start crying, and don't say something sweet and sympathetic because I cain't handle it right now."

"Are you done?"

She slapped me and pounded on my chest and I let her. Then she was crying, clinging to my shirt, and I picked her up and carried her to the sofa, and held her in my lap.

"I spent half my life trying to get him to show me some human damn emotion and now that he does, I just cain't stand it."

"Who?"

"My daddy, who d'you think? And how did you know my momma used to make Brunswick Stew?"

"I didn't. I just...wanted to make something nice..."

"Daddy didn't want me t'use her recipe after she died. I haven't had it in over a decade. You've never made it before."

"I'll throw it out."

"Don't you dare! Hieronymus I love that you cook for me. And I know it's not an empty gesture. I don't know why I said those things."

I wondered how Frank was doing and whether I ought to ask. I sometimes worried that Ethel had only chosen me because being raised by Frank Burkitt had made her think she didn't deserve better. Maybe the truth was more complicated. There was a half-naked stranger in my house, and all I wanted was my wife back.

"I'm okay, Cogbill. We better eat. Are those biscuits?"

In that moment, I confess, I was not sure I loved her.

All through supper as I watched her eat, I was struck by the fact that I did not really know her private thoughts, and that my once-quiet life had become filled with drama and screaming and I had charged blithely into it perhaps to escape my own thoughts and fears. Hell, our courtship, over a year past, had lasted a mere week, and our engagement a matter of months.

She smiled at me across the table and ran her foot up and down my leg. Ethel has always been an intensely sexual being, and I do not deny that it is part of her charm; but I was unaccustomed even in that context to feeling like a piece of meat, although I understood that what she sought was perhaps a release from her own thoughts.

So after supper, instead of doing the dishes we went and lay by the fire, and made love, and I held her and kissed her hair and reminded her that her father's behavior was not her responsibility. As I watched her breathing it came to me that I did not need to know her thoughts, nor she mine; we only needed to know that we could trust one another in good times and bad as we had sworn before our friends and our family and the Lord himself one fine day the previous April. Everything else was manageable.

That night as I slid out of consciousness I entered a world I sometimes saw in the space between dreams and wakefulness; a realm where the air was full of ash and the dead walked among the craggy, colorless rocks, and endless lengths of black fabric rolled from the towers of temples into the slate-colored sky. I was aware of my body, prone in our bed, but I could not move it, and I watched a lonely German child playing in a ditch, his mother standing over him, both of them covered in blood and soot and looking at me disdainfully, and I felt shame and terror that I had not spoken of in two decades. I tried like hell to wake up and found myself still frozen in bed, my eyes screwed shut, third eye wide open, as the blue, ashen face of Nestor Lazos hovered above me, blind eyes and soulless grin, black blood dripping from the cavern in his chest.

"Still livin' the dream, hey Cogbill?"

"Go to hell, Nestor."

And I forced myself awake, jackknifing into a sitting position, the scream in my head escaping as a guttural grunt. Ethel stirred and looked up at me.

"That musta been one heck of a nightmare."

"It was."

"Come here."

She took my head to her chest and stroked my hair.

"We can't fix each other," I said.

"We ain't supposed to, Hieronymus. Reckon we're just supposed to make a space that's safe for the both of us."

"I'm scared that I can't protect you."

"I can handle myself."

"I'm my own worst enemy. The way I feel, every day...I wouldn't wish that on anybody."

"Hey. It's okay. You're not alone."

"I'm not talking about me. Or I am but...today I realized I spend so much time in my own head, I may not be sensitive enough to what's in yours."

"Well you cain't read minds."

"No, but I can read you. I'm just so hardwired to beat myself up that when I feel you being tense I assume it's my fault. And it's not always about me."

"Try being a girl going through puberty with an emotionally constipated widower as your only parent. For a long time I assumed he didn't even care. He just wasn't available, and I thought he was punishing me by withholding his love but now I guess he had some damned macho idea that he couldn't let me see him cry."

I put my arms around her waist and stroked her hip.

"Now he's got emotional sepsis."

She let out a bitter laugh. "Boy, that says it."

"Do you want me to talk to him?"

"I don't think he'll listen."

"I'm the problem."

"Hieronymus you are not the problem."

"To him, I am. Maybe we need to have it out, for your sake, or his sake, or all our sakes."

"Oh, Lord."

"We should try to take him to church on Sunday."

"They don't allow boxing on Sundays."

"That's not in the Bible."

"I'm pretty sure it's the eleventh commandment."

"Ol' Moses must've busted that one off when he come down and had his conniption."

"That's exactly what happened. No boxing on Sundays."

"Yes ma'am."

"Cogbill?"

"Hmm?"

"Hold me tighter."

"Yes ma'am."

CHAPTER NINE

THURSDAY MORNING I was breaking down pallets of freight in the Circle Supermarket stockroom, sorting the freight by category and loading it onto floats to replenish the shelves. Contrary to what most people believe, the stockroom of a supermarket isn't a warehouse, it's a workroom. If you receive regular shipments of freight you don't need to warehouse much of it on site. You want it on the shelves to generate sales, not collecting cobwebs on bunkers in the back.

There's a loading dock, a driver's exit, a receiving workstation, a breakroom, and an office. It needs to be swept daily and the trash taken out at least as often. There are walk-in coolers and freezers, which are functionally holding areas for perishables, and like the stockroom, are mainly used for processing deliveries. It's labor-intensive and we do the best we can.

I was finishing up the first pallet, hefting forty-pound bales of Domino sugar and stacking them on the float for the baking needs section, looking at the next pallet with some trepidation. It was listing about twelve degrees to the left on account of someone at Richfood having stacked the canned goods on top of a case of Corn Flakes, which were now pretty much unsalable due to having buckled under the weight of canned beans and potted meat.

"They should make those warehouse guys come here and break this stuff down."

I was carefully splitting the plastic film from the top few inches of the pallet, knowing I'd have to be slow and cautious to avoid either injuring myself or losing a bunch more product trying to get through this one, when Mr. Clare came and got me.

"I think you ought to hear this."

Something in his tone decided me against asking questions, and I welcomed a break, so I followed him to his office.

The woman's name was Carol Madison, and she was the waitress who had served Ethel and myself the night we had pizza. She looked to be in her late twenties.

"Carol waited tables next door for a few years, then when the pizzeria opened she went there."

"Okay."

"Some of what she said don't really concern you, but, well, I'd feel better if you heard the rest of it."

We sat down in the office. Carol lit up a cigarette and dropped the lighter on Clare's desk.

"Like I told Mr. Clare, Freddy and Ernie aren't good guys."

"They're mixed up with the mob?"

She appeared to be trying to dislodge something from her teeth using her tongue.

"I heard some things. Pieces of conversations. There's a guy called Adagio or something, hangs around sometimes, I think they work for him."

"Hector Adagio, yeah, I know him."

"And a big guy with manners like an ape. The way he looks at me, at all of us. Makes me feel dirty. I heard them talking about you."

"Me?"

"Mr. Clare says you're Mr. Cogbill."

I swallowed and uncrossed my legs.

"They said my name?"

She nodded and took a long drag on her cigarette. There was an office in back of The Ernest Pie where the Vittorio brothers did their accounting, and Hector Adagio had the use of it when he was in town. The previous evening the Irishman had plowed through the front door of the little pizzeria, the cowbell flailing wildly, the dinner crowd looking up in surprise at the rude manner of the big red-faced man as he bulled his way to the counter. Even the Jukebox seemed to pause George Jones. A teenage waitress nearly dropped her tray as he shoved past her, and rather than apologize he slapped her behind and steamrolled on.

"Sorry honey. Hey, Hector here?"

"Will you shuddup?"

Fred Vittorio showed him to the office.

"Whyn't you announce to the whole fucking world why you're in town?"

"Relax, Hector, these rednecks don't give a shit about us."

"I told you before, you address me as Mr. Adagio. You got that?"

"Right."

"Any sign of DiRossi or not?"

"Nah he ain't coming back. The feds are watching the place."

"They didn't see you, did they?"

"Will you relax? Your ass was any tighter you could shit through a keyhole."

Carol had a partial angle past the prep area. She took one quick nervous glance and saw Adagio's mouth pull into a straight line, his eyes narrowing as he regarded the Irishman. He took a slow, deep breath through flaring nostrils. "What's your next move?"

"I got one lead. There was some guy in a Pontiac pulled up, talked to the feds."

"Cogbill. Guy's a pain the ass. Ran Jimmie Vasiliou out of here last year. His wife clipped Nestor Lazos."

"Nestor the Lizard got popped by some redneck gash?"

"Yeah, they grow 'em different down here."

"No shit. Try Florida, place is a open-air lunatic asylum."

"Yeah, my first wife was one of the inmates. Cogbill knows Tony and the Johnson kid. He's a nosy fucker, but as a snoop he's amateur hour."

"He's all we got to go on."

"So watch him. He told me Tony was no friend of his, now you're telling me he's at his house. Maybe he's holding out."

"Whyn't I just snatch him, beat the dope out of him, ace him and be done with it?"

"Because he ain't worth the trouble."

"Trouble? I'm about all the trouble he can take."

"I said no."

"What'd your Florida bitch run off wit' yer dork?"

"Look, I don't need some harp fucker telling me my business, you got that, Feeley?"

"Sure thing, Hector."

"That's Mr. Adagio."

"Sure thing. Hector."

The big Irishman charged out of the office, plowed into Carol, cupped her breast as he caught her, and smiled at her with pink, curling lips and eyes like wet coal.

"Ain't mean to cop a feel there. Long as we're acquainted, lemme buy you a Coke."

When Carol finished telling the story, she stubbed out the cigarette and wiped tears from her eyes.

"Don't go back there," I said.

"That's why I'm here. I want my old job back."

Clare's face registered genuine concern.

"You're welcome back any time. But maybe you ought to talk to Jay Powell."

"And tell him what? Grown men were using foul language? I overheard a guy tell another guy not to hurt someone. Maybe he accidentally touched my breast when he almost knocked me down."

"You know that's not true."

"Does it matter? It's his word against mine. I'm just some hysterical woman."

Maybe I should have taken Mahoney's warnings more seriously. Maybe I should have listened to Jay Powell. The truth is, there are two main ways we deal with things that frighten or otherwise discomfort us. One is to panic and go into a frenzy of activity that rarely produces anything of value. The other is to avoid looking directly at the offensive subject and occupy ourselves with that which we believe we can control.

That evening as Jay Powell settled in at home, the telephone rang and he put down his bottle and the newspaper he was reading and glared at it. When it persisted, he hoisted himself up and lifted it from the cradle.

"Sheriff, this' Ronnie Jett at the Rappahannock Regional Jail. I got a State Trooper here arrested a feller for drunk driving."

"Well if one of you boys looking for a commendation you done got the wrong number."

"Driver's from King George."

"Say again?"

"He insisted I should call you."

"Well son, what in Christ is his name?"

"Errr..." some paper shuffled down the line. "Clare. Logan Veola Clare."

"I'll be there in twenty. And don't do nothing damned stupid in the meantime, like press charges."

"Sir?" But Powell had disconnected the call.

Jay put his uniform shirt back on and tucked it in and combed his hair, put on his gun and his jacket and laid his hat crown down on the backseat of his car. He hit the bubble light and booked ass for Fredericksburg, the siren wailing like damnation over stubbled fields in the empty country night.

Half an hour later he was heading back to Willow Hill with an indignant Vee Clare in the passenger seat.

"Never been so damned humiliated in all my life."

"Now Vee you know them Staties is new. They ain't learned yet how we operate."

Clare was not an habitual drinker but every once in a while he was known to go "on a toot," and it was Powell's custom, and that of the previous Troopers, to see to it he got home safely.

"Trifling bastard arrested me in my own driveway. Followed me home and did it right in my own driveway with my wife watching."

"Ain't like she didn't know you was drinking."

"S'not the point, Jay. Not the point at all. Some things are supposed to be sacred. Untouchable. Now that was my private property."

"Ol' boy thought you were running. Now we'll straighten it out tomorrow."

Clare watched the pale moonlight wash across the fields at Burnley and felt the tires rumble over the railroad tracks at Farley Vale.

"Jay, you ever get the feeling that maybe sometime when we wasn't looking, evil done moved in?"

"You ain't talking about that ol' Trooper no more, is you?"

Clare unconsciously fingered a spot on his head where a young man had sapped him in the parking lot at Little Reno a couple years before, when the slots still ran, and he'd won big, only to have the prize money stolen from him as he unlocked his car.

"Other things and maybe that too. I don't know. They think we're simple country bumpkins and they can take advantage of our kindness and our relaxed way of living and hurt women and children right under our noses and take advantage of black folks, and maybe we won't notice or care."

"You're starting to sound like Cogbill. Evil been creepin' round the garden since Adam and Eve. You cain't dwell on it or it'll swallow you up."

"What worries me is the thought that while we been not dwelling on it, it done put up a house."

They were passing Hop Yard Farm and Rokeby and coming up on Jeter's Lumber Mill and Clare's home at Arnold's Corner. When they pulled up to Willow Hill, all the lights were on and Clare's car sat in the driveway like a junebug, parked at an angle, the driver-side window down. The front door of the proud old antebellum home swung open and Mrs. Clare stepped out onto the wide, columned porch.

"You just get inside and sleep it off, Vee. See if things don't look better when the sun come up tomorrow."

CHAPTER TEN

I WAS STANDING outside Stuckey's on 301 just north of Office Hall, huddled into a payphone and drinking coffee out of a thermos. It occurred to me that if I was going to start doing this sort of thing regularly it might behoove me to get a telephone. Or an office. Or both: I supposed there was little point in an office without a telephone.

I listened to the click and hum as the line connected and an attractive-sounding female voice spoke.

"K Department."

"Ah, yes, I'm calling for Miss Laura Dawson?"

"Speaking."

"Miss Dawson? My name is Harry Cogbill, I'm working for Mildred Harris. Dane's wife? I wondered if it would be possible to ask you a few questions."

"Mr. Cogbill, yes. Mrs. Harris told me you might call. I'm not sure how I can help you."

A woman in a flannel coat and wool hat tapped on the glass and I raised a hand to signal her I wouldn't be long. She appeared rather harried and was towing a chubby-faced kid who just now resembled a screaming tomato.

"Maybe you noticed some things, or maybe you have some insight since you worked with him. Would it be possible to do this in person? I'm on a payphone."

"I can meet you at the Post Office on my lunch break. You know where it is?"

"Outside the main gate, yes ma'am."

"Great. Say eleven o'clock?"

I heard the coin drop when I hung up the phone, and stepped out of the booth where the woman was fussing over the disconsolate child, and headed through the pecan shop to use the men's room. A few moments later I was tending to some personal business when in my peripheral vision, a large man walked up to the next urinal and stood there sighing loudly as his stream whooshed against the porcelain, as though the pleasure afforded him by his urination was almost sexual in nature. I zipped up and flushed with my elbow, turning for the sink.

"You ever notice how many boogies there are on the tile above a urinal?"

I looked back at the pissing man and recognized him as the Irish hitter from Florida who had barged into the Circle Family Restaurant. His neck was hunched into his round shoulders, his chin tucked in, feet well apart, his spine arched, hands on his lower back, trilby pulled low over his eyes. His cheeks were pink as gala apples as he turned his face to me and smiled, a toothpick protruding from the corner of his mouth. It was the smile of a predator, the way a rapist might regard an unaccompanied girl or a mainline con a fresh-faced inmate. I did not respond to him, but twisted the handles of the faucet. The Irishman put away his piece and turned away from the urinal without flushing.

"Could just flick 'em in the pisser, y'know? Guys are lazy. Once at a gas station outside Sarasota I saw a turd in a urinal." He was still smiling intently at me as he said it. He didn't blink, and as he approached the sink I left the restroom. I believe he was attempting to intimidate me, and I felt the best course was to pretend I didn't notice the tactic at all. Many times in the years since, I have wondered if I should have played it differently, and if doing so might have prevented some of the worst of what followed. But second-guessing myself is one of the more useless and destructive aspects of my nature.

At ten-fifty-two I was parked in front of the big neoclassical Dahlgren Post Office, listening to the pulleys on the flagpole rattling in the cool breeze while a bored guard at the gate read a paperback and drank something warm out of his own thermos and when need arose, checked badges and stickers and waved cars past his little glass box onto land where Elijah Taylor's daddy had raised chickens and grown vegetables and played outfield on a community baseball team.

At five after eleven a sporty little coupe eased out past the guardhouse and made a left turn into the post office. The girl driving it was blonde and close to Ethel's age. She was wearing a suit, a skirt and jacket combo in pale blue that brought out her eyes. She had on flats and a tasteful gold chain and a dainty wristwatch and a wrap that probably wasn't real fur. Her hair was curled and if those weren't false eyelashes it was a miracle none of her girlfriends had shot her. She swelled and tapered in all the places a fellow likes to see, and I wondered how many times a day she had to field unwanted advances.

"Are you Laura Dawson?"

"Mr. Cogbill?"

"Harry, please."

We shook hands.

"Are you a mathematician?"

"Would that shock you Mr. Cogbill?"

"No ma'am. Although we've only just met. I've only met two other mathematicians that I am aware of and they were both very awkward men."

"Dane and Maynard? Well in fact my degree's in math, but I'm afraid here I mostly make coffee and answer phones. That's probably not the conversation you came here to have."

It wasn't, and I wasn't sure where to go with that, so I cleverly chose to ignore it.

"What was your impression of Dane?"

"Smart. Uncomfortable around other men. I think he felt challenged by them."

"Challenged in what way?"

"Insecure. Like he didn't think he measured up."

"To Maynard Carter?"

"Maybe not Maynard, but some of the others."

"Did Dane ever behave inappropriately toward you?"

"Oh heavens, no. Dane wasn't like that. He was a very nice man. Sweet, gentle. I think his home life had been difficult."

Whose wasn't? "Yeah, I had the impression he and Millie were having problems."

"I meant his life growing up. He never felt he fit in, even here. But he wanted to. Desperately."

"He told you that?"

"Parts of it. Other parts I had to kind of fill in, you know?"

"You knew him pretty well?"

"I wouldn't say that, no."

"But he talked about his childhood to you?"

"A little. I guess he was lonely."

"He had a wife at home."

"Like you said, they were having trouble."

"You're sure there was nothing between you two?"

"I don't appreciate your tone. I wasn't attracted to him, nor him to me."

Having seen both of them, I believed half of that was true.

"Who was he attracted to?"

She drew in her breath, and I saw her nostrils whiten.

"One assumes, his wife."

Remembering the last time I'd seen Dane, I wasn't so sure.

"Can I call you again if I think of anything more I'd like to ask you?"

"I'm not so sure I'd appreciate that, Mr. Cogbill. I really don't know what else I can tell you."

There was some answer she'd left unsaid, but I didn't know what the question was, and like many pretty young women she had erected some type of force-shield that she deployed whenever talking one-on-one with an older man. Which made her connection with Dane all the more curious.

That afternoon since I wasn't working, Ethel and I drove west across the rolling hills of corn stubble dotted with barns the color of tarnished silver, to the boyhood home of Washington below the hanging stench of the cellophane plant, and then under the railroad tracks and over the Chatham Bridge across the Rappahannock into downtown Fredericksburg. We parked near the river in a gravel lot off Sophia Street (pronounced to rhyme with Mariah) and walked around the block, Amelia to Caroline, to the Victoria Theater with its art deco façade and shimmering marquee advertising a feature starring Bob Hope and Lucille Ball.

I do not deny that my tastes ran more to noir or western, but Ethel wanted a romantic comedy and as she often said, you take the good with the bad. Still, I could have passed up a film about two people who fall in love while married to other people, and I couldn't help but think about Dane and Mildred, and the pretty miss Dawson, and I wondered what it was that she had elected not to tell me. She knew so much about Dane, as if she'd had long, intimate conversations with him. He'd gotten past her defenses. Bald, bespectacled, socially-inept Dane Harris. Was he the kind of guy to use the authority of his position to elicit sex from a secretary? Maybe Mildred was right. Their marriage had been difficult. She berated him. He was lonely, seeking connection. It was there, around the edges of what Laura Dawson had said.

After the movie, we walked a short distance down Caroline Street, my collar turned up and my hat pulled low against the wind; Ethel in her green coat and bell-like hat clinging to my arm. We sat on vinyl stools in Goolrick's as we had on one of our first dates, and hung our coats and hats on hooks beneath the counter.

"Wasn't that a cute picture? I told you it'd be cute."

"Sure," I said.

"You didn't like it."

"Ethel I'm glad you had a nice time, that's all that matters."

"You really want to watch Stanley Baker chase after a killer for an hour and a half?"

"Why not?"

"Movies are supposed to be an escape, Cogbill."

"It's set in London."

"It's a detective movie. You don't think that hits a little too close to home?"

"I'm a stock boy."

"You're an ass." She poked me in the arm.

"Well, that too. Besides, Bob and Lucy got me thinking about Dane Harris, so the way I look at it, I still didn't get an escape."

"You think Dane was cheating?"

"I met the K Department secretary today. Laura Dawson."

"Oh?"

"She seemed awfully well-acquainted with Dane's child-hood, his personality, his insecurities."

"Uh-oh."

"Yeah."

"Is she pretty?"

"Yep."

"Like, give Dane a heart attack pretty?"

"Probably. I mean, I don't know what her lovers get to see."

"Yeah, well, try not to imagine too hard."

"She isn't my type."

"What type is that?"

"You."

She leaned her head on my shoulder.

"I'm sorry I keep being such a bitch to you, Cogbill."

"Don't ever say that."

"What, that I'm sorry for being a bitch?"

"Don't say you're a bitch."

"Well, but I can be one sometimes."

"Maybe I'm just an old man with old-fashioned ideas."

"Hey, don't you go saying a thing like that, either. You're not old. You're older than me but you are not old."

"You deserve better."

"Y'know I have dated other men. Younger men. Before I met you."

"I know."

"I didn't marry them."

"I know that too."

"Because it turned out they were just boys."

"Meaning what?"

"They couldn't handle me, the same way your girlfriends could never handle you."

"Aren't we a hell of a pair?"

"Hieronymus we're the best there is, and don't you forget it."

What could I say to that?

On the way home from Fredericksburg, Ethel and I stopped by John's store in Gera to pick up our mail.

"Cogbill, that fella from Boston called for you."

"Len Mahoney?"

"Yeah. Sounded important. Wants you should call him."

When Len picked up, he sounded tired.

"Got a visit from the feds yesterday."

"Hey, you're the one that called them."

"Yeah, but I didn't expect the third degree. They asked some funny questions though. You met a guy named Eamon Feeley?"

"Should I have?"

"Hell no. Based on the fact they asked me about him, I'm assuming it's the same Eamon Feeley I went to school with, but that was a long time ago."

"High School reunion?"

"Look, how many guys you remember from high school?"

"A few."

"Right. A few. Some faces without names, some names without faces. I don't remember the names of all the guys who sat at my lunch table. I can't remember the face of the first girl I kissed. But I remember Eamon Feeley."

"That's great, Len. What's this got to do with me?"

"I'm getting there. It was a Catholic school we went to. He used to drive the nuns up the wall, they couldn't control him. He'd cuss at the priest. And he was a big kid, Cogbill. I mean a fuckin' huge kid, and meaner than he was big. He stove another kid's head in over a nickel. One of the nuns got hurt trying to break up the fight, she was on oxygen the rest of her life. Wasn't ever the same."

"A real model youth, then."

"Yeah. They expelled him, and a couple weeks later some of the guys saw him working at a butcher shop up the block. I guess he apprenticed there and after they bombed Pearl he went in the Navy. I never saw him again. I remember the look on his face after the fight that day, though. He thought it was funny."

It finally clicked into place for me.

"He's been in Florida."

"Thought you hadn't met him."

"Well, I think I was wrong."

"I put it together from the questions they asked me. I don't know any Palm Beach cops but I managed to make a union connection through my Uncle Barry. He retired down there and does some work for the DA. Turns out Feeley has been on the Job in Palm Beach for years, only he's suspended on account of some bad gambling debts."

"He's a sadist hiding behind a badge and that's what they finally got him on? Gambling debts?"

"You know how it is. Union protects him because that's their job. IAB does an investigation in the dark with a bag over their head, 'whoops, sorry, nothing to see here,' and the guy skates."

"Probably moonlights as an enforcer, right?"

"That'd be my guess. And with all the debt hanging over him, the local greaseballs own his entire ass."

"Thanks for the heads-up."

"One other thing. He's been in Florida since he got out the Navy. He's a hunter. Probably just likes killing things, right? Reason I'm telling you, he's an outdoorsman. He's not one of those city guys lost in the sticks, out of his element. He's used to swamps and forests. You get me?"

"Yeah Len, I get you."

I heard him sigh.

"Cogbill, I know you ain't gonna leave this alone, but I wish you would. Feeley's evil. Let the feds and the local sheriff deal with it, just keep your head down and think about your wife, will ya?"

Later as my Pontiac bumped down our driveway, the setting sun bathing our fields in fire, the lengthening shadows reaching like dark fingers pointing toward Index and the distant abode of Tom Boone, I watched a dozen blackbirds erupt from the canopy of the forest beyond the gardens and the yards where turkeys often rooted for snails and iridescent grackles congregated in spring.

I wondered briefly what had spooked the birds, but thought nothing of it until that night when Ethel pulled the curtains to undress for bed, and called me to our room.

"What is it?"

"I think I saw a light in the woods."

I turned out the bedroom light, waited for my eyes to adjust, then got down my Army field-glasses from the closet. The moonlight shone pale and cold around the edges of the curtain. Carefully, I slipped behind the curtains and stared across the field. There was an orange glow out among the trees.

I peered through the glasses and after a bit of fumbling, I found the glow.

"Looks like fire."

"Oh Lord, is it a wildfire?"

"I think it's a campfire."

"Maybe just some kids, then."

"Maybe."

But I was thinking about the missing William Johnson, Joey breaking into our house, and the big Irishman who had busted into the Circle Family Restaurant looking for the Vittorios. Eamon Feeley. Agent Douglas telling me there was a lot going on that I didn't know about.

"I better go check it out. Lock all the doors, don't open them for anybody but me."

"Hieronymus, take the shotgun."

"I want you to have it, just in case."

"I ain't opening any doors this time, Cogbill."

"I'm not leaving you here unarmed."

"Your pistol's in a safe deposit box near the courthouse and you cain't get to it 'til morning. Take the damn shotgun."

I wanted to refuse. I hated leaving her unarmed. But her tone said the matter was settled and I did not want to fight. I pulled all the drapes in the house, got my coat and hat, and made sure the shotgun was loaded. I stuffed extra shells in my coat pockets, then turned out all the lights, stepped onto the front porch, and waited to hear the bolt slide shut in the door behind me.

I crept around the side of the house to the backyard, keeping low, and followed along the fences wrapped in the woody snares of vines going into hibernation for the winter. It wasn't much cover but it was about all our property afforded me. The edge of the forest was thick with wild blackberries and devil's walking-stick, and saplings of oak and maple, little more than sticks in the sleeping autumn wild.

But I knew the paths, made by deer as they traveled foraging for food, and under the molting canopy the spaces between the trees were ample, barring the occasional greenbrier or feeble twist of holly. I moved slowly, taking the quietest route, and had to travel fifty yards along a creekbed to a place where a long-forgotten barbed-wire fence had been swallowed by two tree-trunks and cut away between them to create a kind of im-promptu gate.

I drew near enough to have a good view of the campsite where I crouched behind the trunk of a large beech. A small man sat under a makeshift tent, really just a tarp or a shower curtain stretched across some low branches and propped with a few sticks. I couldn't see his face, but he had his hands in his coat-pockets and a bottle of brandy at his feet. There was a tin percolator near the fire and a couple of enamel cups hanging off branches near the tarp. He shivered, and reached for the brandy.

"You know that's just gonna lower your body-temperature."

He jumped up, knocking down the sticks, the tarp flopping over his head like a child's Halloween costume. I stood up and strode out from behind the tree with the shotgun leveled at the frantic figure. He swore and flailed comically as he fought his way out of the tarp, and between the accent and the obvious limp I wasn't surprised when the face of Joey DeLarosa emerged from the rustling plastic.

"Jesus God, Cogbill!"

"What are you doing out here?"

"Trynna lay low is what, I got problems but you ain't seem to care too much so I hadda handle it myself." His clothes were filthy and he hadn't shaved in some time.

"Yeah you look like you got everything pretty well nailed down here."

"You still sore 'cos I came in your house?"

"Uninvited, in the bedroom where my wife sleeps, yeah. Yeah I'm not really thrilled about that sort of thing."

"I already toldja I ain't mean nothing by that."

"I know who you are."

There was a long pause.

"I thought we'd established that."

"Antonio DiRossi."

He laughed nervously and put his hands up.

"Ah Christ. They got to you, didn't they?"

"Who's 'they,' Tony?"

"That wop lawyer, who else?"

"Adagio."

"Yeah, the mob fixer from Brooklyn. Look I don't know if the reward's higher if I'm alive, but I think I'd prefer if you just shoot me and get it over with."

"You tipped off a rival outfit to a mob shipment. What was Adagio importing?"

"I didn't see nothing, awright? I was too busy shittin' my pants. That's what you want to hear, ain't it?"

"What I want to hear is the truth."

"That is the truth, Hare. I'm sorry. Shoot me if you wanna."

"They didn't get to me. Joey."

"Then what are you doin' out here?"

"In case you haven't noticed, the leaves are starting to fall, and that campfire's visible from pretty far away."

"Aw fuck."

"I didn't figure a city boy like you would know how to make a campfire."

"They got Boy Scouts in New York, wiseass." He saluted me with the wrong number of fingers.

"That's not even the Scout salute."

"Whatever. Point is I got nowhere to go."

"You have a car. You can go literally anywhere."

"Adagio seen my heap. Besides, I got other concerns."

"The feds want you."

"That's why I like you, Cogbill. You don't miss much."

"They're looking for you. Watching your house."

"Yeah, I'm lucky I gave 'em the slip."

"Lucky?"

"They can't protect me, Hare. Nobody can."

"Where's your wife and kids, Joey?"

"Ah, that was just a bunch a malarkey, Hare."

"Was it? Tell me you put them on a train in Fredericksburg and sent them far, far away."

"Like I said, you don't miss much. They're safer away from me."

"Well you can't sleep in the woods forever."

"Tell me about it. Too many sounds out here, it's creepy. Colder than a witch's titty, too."

"You don't have a plan, do you?"

"I'm working on it."

"Yeah? Well work on it someplace else. You're endangering my wife being this close to my house."

"Endangering? Shit, even the bears are scared of her."

"Why are you this close to my house?"

"I never meant for none a this to happen, Hare. We got behind on the house payments, I borrowed money from a guy in Jersey. Only now instead of the bank riding my ass I got some Genovese flunky trying to wring me out. That damn phone call was supposed to cancel my debt."

"I don't think those guys are in the business of canceling debts, Joey."

"Tell me about it. I didn't know all those guys was gonna get killed. Christ, it was horrible. I still see it in my sleep. And now instead of Genovese or the bank it's the damn FBI bending me over. I'm getting screwed raw."

"You made your own choices, Joey. They were lousy, but they're all yours. What the hell are you thinking dragging me and my wife into it?"

"You got kind of a reputation for being a stick-it-to-the-man type, is all."

"So you thought I'd help you?"

"Yeah. Yeah, I thought you was standup. What can I say, I'm a lousy judge a character. Then that bitch wife a yours knocks me on my ass and you gimme the ol' heave-ho."

I slugged him across the jaw and he went down like Howdy Doody on Frank Paris's smoke break.

"Don't you talk about her like that."

"Jesus, you deserve each other."

"You're goddamned right we do."

"Okay, okay. I'll get outta here tomorrow, I promise. It's too dark tonight, right?"

"I'm coming back in the morning. Don't be here."

I slept very little. I held Ethel in my arms and listened to the sounds of the old house settling, a whippoorwill in the field and the rasping shriek of a juvenile barred owl in the ancient poplar beside the house. Periodically, Fawkes came in and leapt upon the bed, making small noises as he snuffled about my face, and disappeared again into the darkened house.

I rose at dawn, disentangling myself from Ethel's warm embrace, started the coffee to percolate while I dressed. I took the shotgun and locked the door behind me, and retraced my steps to Joey's campsite. He was gone and he'd taken everything with him, which should have made me feel better, except I noticed two different sets of footprints excluding my own from the night before, little Joey's uneven gait and small feet, and a much larger set of prints mingling with them, sometimes under mine, and sometimes over them. I remembered then that there had been two coffee cups hanging by the tarp. Why two cups?

The same reason as Dane Harris: he wasn't alone. Although I doubted Joey or whatever the hell his name was, was in the forest with a secretary, no matter how beautiful. The city boy had a guide, and I'd blundered right past him in the dark. Whoever was with him had watched me come in the night before, and leave again, and never made a sound.

Could it have been Feeley? It seemed unlikely. Unless I hadn't given Joey enough credit for bravery or acting ability, there's just no way he wouldn't have given a sign. Outside the campsite, the leaf cover was too thick and I couldn't tell which way they'd gone. But Joey had to have left his car someplace. He couldn't have gotten it far from a road or driveway of some type. The options would be limited. I'd make breakfast and then go for a drive.

Halfway back to the house, it crossed my mind that the second man in the forest might have been William Johnson. They had worked together. They had problems with the same people.

They both needed to disappear. They both knew me. William was my friend, and Joey thought he was my friend. I'd been so cross at Joey that I hadn't really given him a chance to say anything of consequence. Maybe breakfast could wait. Maybe I'd better skip straight to the drive.

CHAPTER ELEVEN

THE RAIN was a grey, icy mist that hung in the air like judgment as the Pontiac bore me south along the pale, narrow ribbon of Millbank Road. There were only a few places anyone could leave a car and end up in the woods behind my house, and all the options were farms. The most likely one was an abandoned house that sat alone in a field not far from Frank's place.

I turned off Millbank onto a farm road buried in drifts of wet leaves faded to dull rust, the spines of hibernating trees glistening black and grey all around me. A young fawn stood in the road watching me approach, and leapt, spring-loaded, into the brush. Where the forest opened up to golden corn stubble, I was forced to stop in the road while a fat tom turkey barred the way, his snood, wattle, and necktie swaying, blue head held erect, chest puffed, tail fanned, his blunt, shingled feathers of copper and charcoal ruffling against the cold as his harem of two-dozen dull-colored hens trundled across the road. It was almost Thanksgiving and I had a shotgun, but what he didn't know wouldn't hurt him today.

Ahead, a kettle of vultures circled low in the dreary sky, above the hunched shapes of their colleagues gathered on the rise. As I drove up the feeding committee scattered, huge wings beating the air and settling in the trees until I passed. One or two of the big black buzzards sat on the fences watching intently.

As I passed by the carcass, I could see it was a mid-size doe, her skin rent and peeled back, grey bones and red sinew laid bare to the sky. A hunter might have taken a bad shot, though she likely had been no prize either for show or game. Someone could have struck her out on Millbank or Port Conway Road, or even Route 3 or 301. A wounded deer will run some distance before she collapses and dies. But I did wonder if it might not be something else.

I didn't know who owned the property, but someone did because the fields were maintained, though not with the kind of care I'd expect if the old homestead were still in use. The fields were irregular, the shape of the clearing just sort of a formless blotch, if squarer and more symmetrical than my own.

Up on a rise was a cluster of trees draped in grapevine, a few tufts of juniper and cedar, and the thrawn shapes of holly and greenbrier the only faint splatter of green. In the middle of the trees was the grey husk of a building canted to the right, resembling less a house in its present state than Noah's Ark run aground, the beam of the roof broken in, the ribbed tin like a dried beech leaf, brown, shriveled and bowed.

I parked a couple hundred yards away and loaded the shotgun. I sat there a while, waiting, searching for any sign of activity. Behind me the vultures resumed their wake. It could be that someone had driven through here recently, and in a hurry, pulverized the poor doe and left her to the buzzards. If that was true, and if I was right about Joey leaving his car here, then the question was, was it Joey that hit the deer, or somebody looking for Joey? And was he on his way in, or out?

I took some small comfort in the fact that the feeding vultures meant there were no larger bodies to feed on in the immediate area. At least not out in the open. When twenty minutes had passed, and the vultures had come to blows over the remains of the doe, I drove slowly up to the ruins on the rise. Where the farm track ended I could faintly see the twin silver lines of tire tracks leading around the building.

The back side of the house was gone. Inside, I could see the plaster had collapsed off the buckling walls and the wood slats warped and twisted beneath the sagging weight of the house. The remaining furniture sat rotting, the last scraps of a forgotten life. In days past I had been visited by the dead, seen them walk and heard their voices like faint radio chatter echo from beyond the veil. I have never been sure if these things were real or imagined, but I was certain that nothing good or wholesome ever came from hanging around a place like this, and no words spoken by any who dwelt among these shadows would bring wisdom or tidings that the living should ever wish to hear.

I took a deep breath, grabbed the shotgun, and got out of the car. The house could fall at any moment, though surely the worst had already occurred. The floor of the porch had collapsed but the supports, to the extent they supported anything, still stood. The brush was flattened out, the saplings bent or broken off. Tire treads had left an impression in the mud. Someone had stepped in turkey scat. There was broken glass on the ground. Not the wavy, bubbly kind that had once filled the panes of the house, but modern glass. Smooth, clear, faintly green. A car window.

Might be nothing. Some kids might have found the car. Joey was a klutz. Or Feeley might have been here, looking for clues. If he had better tracking skills than I did, he might have found their campsite. And from there, my house. No, no. If he killed anyone in the woods he didn't leave the bodies, or the vultures would be on them by now, and he couldn't have driven out in both vehicles. So either he wasn't here, he'd already been and left, or he wasn't alone and they took Joey, his friend, and his car. Maybe Joey was never even here. Maybe someone drove up here looking for antiques to salvage, broke a window out of their vehicle loading some furniture, and drove away.

I walked to the edge of the forest and looked around a few minutes. Under an ancient sweet gum tree, a path led into the forest. Where the gumballs were scattered, a few were flattened or ground into the mud. Some of the leaf-cover was turned over. Birds and squirrels will do that, foraging for food, but they don't leave boot-prints and they certainly don't drop enameled tin coffee cups like the one I found there, in a shallow puddle. It was speckled and blue, and matched the ones I'd seen at Joey's campsite the night before. Of course, they were available in pretty much any sporting goods store. I had one myself, and had taken my coffee in it every day for years.

I could keep trying to talk myself out of it. It was hunters, campers, scavengers. Or I could admit that my gut was right, that Joey and possibly William Johnson had been here, had left in a hurry, had some kind of confrontation, and someone had broken a window out of Joey's car. I had no idea where they'd gone. I walked back to my car and drove away. When the vultures scattered again, I stopped and looked in the farm track near the place where the doe had fallen. Ground into the mud was a broken piece of plastic in the shape of a stretched out red, white, and blue escutcheon.

One of the turkey buzzards screamed at me from his guard post on the fence, and his wings made an impressive whooshing sound as he flapped them at me a couple of times. I got back in the Pontiac and dropped the little plastic shield on the passenger seat. It was a stylized heraldic crest, alternating fields of blank white and fields of red with small gold fleurs-de-lis, a blue bowtie in the middle. The insert from the hood insignia of a Chevrolet Bel Air. It was cracked, and muddy. Maybe Joey had been in a hurry because of me. Maybe the broken window really was innocent. Some kids had found it while exploring, or Joey had an accident packing the car.

Maybe Joey and William were in trouble, or worse, beyond help. I had to think. The first question was whether William was acting as Joey's guide. That was at least partly the case, since William knew the county and had successfully avoided arrest for weeks, and as far as I'd ever been able to tell, Joey was lucky he knew his way around his own trousers.

That brought up another problem. There were, out of custom and necessity, insular black communities throughout the county that William might have allies within. Black-only diners and clubs I'd never be able to set foot in without causing a stir. Nobody would talk to me. If Rollie Taylor were alive, he could be my partner in my non-existent firm, but he wasn't. I liked his father, and I knew there were siblings. But I had no stomach to drag the Taylors into this.

One such diner was the Red Top Grill. It stood at the corner of 301 and Hanover Church Road, near Ralph Bunche School. But it had closed its doors a few years before, and now was an office that sold trailer homes. Still, I knew the man who had owned it, and where to find him.

The driveway went up a rise and blossomed at the end into a loop surrounding Willow Hill. The house sat maybe a hundred yards back from Route 3; once it had been a large white colonial with a wide front gallery and towering brick chimneys at each end, the mortar speckled with lichen and the tin roof gleaming in the sun, the home of Dr. Thomas Thornton Arnold. Vee

IN THE TRACKLESS WILD | 135

Clare had another vision, though: the white clapboard had been replaced with red brick.

The roof and supports had been removed from the front gallery, and replaced with four huge white columns that ran the height of both stories, supporting a new extension to the roof that sat too low over the second floor windows, making the house seem to frown at me as I rattled up the drive. A triangular pediment had been added above the transom window over the front door.

"Why Harry," Clare said when he opened the door. "This is a surprise. Come in, come in."

I stood awkwardly in the front hall with my actual hat in my hands. "I'm sorry to come calling unexpectedly. It's about work. Ah, my other work."

"The investigator thing."

"Right."

"Well that's exciting. Not sure how I can help."

"I'm worried about William Johnson. It occurs to me that if he's hiding somewhere in the county it's not a white man who's going to find him."

"I reckon not."

"You have connections, right? From the Red Top days?"

"Hell, I got all kinds of colored friends. But like you said, if any one of them know where Johnson is they not about to give him up."

"I don't need to know where he is. I just want to know he's safe. And to get a message to him if possible."

"I'll see what I can do. It may take a while."

"I understand."

When I left Willow Hill, I headed West on 3, onto the loop of old Route 3 that went past Comorn house and turned onto the road beside it that headed towards 218 and the home of Mildred Harris. Halfway to 218 I made a right turn onto an unpaved, forested road awash in the autumn detritus, a long driveway that ended in barbed wire fences and fields surrounding a knoll, atop which sat a couple of gnarled, weathered trees and an ancient two-story frame house in pale yellow clapboard, twin brick chimneys touching the sky, a plume of smoke issuing from one; the half-hipped roof plated with green-painted tin, eaves lined with dentils, a large pediment over a protruding front porch, wide gallery in back, and a kitchen attached to one side.

Its name was Marmion. It was built by Colonel William Fitzhugh in 1674, and later belonged to George Washington Lewis, nephew of George Washington and an officer in the Continental Army. According to local legend, during the Revolutionary War a Fitzhugh found a wounded Hessian on the banks of the Potomac and brought him to Marmion to nurse him back to health. The soldier repaid this kindness by painting the parlor, and the paneling he decorated with breathtaking scenes of country life has, since 1913, been on display in New York's Metropolitan Museum of Art.

Just now, the current owner was chopping wood around back. When I got out of the car I could smell the wood smoke from the chimney and the ozone in the air, and Jay Powell lowered his ax, mopping his brow with a kerchief.

"You up early this morning, Cogbill. Get you some coffee? About ready for a cold drink myself."

"I think Joey DeLarosa is in King George. And I think he's in danger."

"Well now what in the hell is he doing here?"

"Hiding. But I found him, and I think maybe somebody else did, too."

"The feds?"

"A button man out of Florida."

"The one showed his butt in the Circle Restaurant?"

"His name's Eamon Feeley. He's from Boston originally."

"How do you know that? Never mind, I don't want to know. Where's DeLarosa at right now?"

"I don't know. He was out in the woods between my house and the Morgan place, but he's gone now. I found this."

I gave him the escutcheon off the Bel Air.

"Well goddamn, DeLarosa got the only known Bel Air in existence."

"I spoke to him, Sheriff. He was there. This is off his car. He left in a hurry, hit a deer. There was broken glass back where he'd parked the car, behind the ruins near the Morgan place. Automotive glass."

I didn't want to tell him about William. I wasn't sure I was right, and I didn't want to get William caught.

"It's a green '53 Bel Air. Missing its hood insignia and at least one window. How hard can it be to find?"

"Pretty hard."

"Sheriff..."

"I know. I'll make some calls."

I couldn't think of anything else I could do to find Joey and William, so I decided to work on the Dane Harris thing for a little while. Since interviewing Laura Dawson, I had more questions for Maynard Carter. I called K Department on the Naval Base, and pretended I wasn't me when Miss Dawson answered the phone. Maynard had taken a personal day. I drove out to his house in Eden Estates, but found myself sitting in the car a short distance up the street, watching.

The Nomad was in the driveway. The family mover, the one you use when you're hauling kids. So whatever Maynard had called out for, it probably wasn't a family emergency.

The Falcon was missing. The compact. A car that screamed Maynard Carter's name if anything did. But the kids would be in school, and maybe his wife would take the Ford to run errands while Maynard stayed home sick. I walked up to the house and rang the bell. Maynard's wife appeared after a moment. Her hair and makeup were done, and although I could see the circles under her eyes she'd evidently tried to cover them. She was all put together, simple jewelry and a dress that flattered her figure. The model of suburbia.

She kept the storm door shut, and made sure it was locked.

"What do you want?"

"I was looking for Maynard, Mrs. Carter."

"Well naturally he's at work."

She seemed nervous.

"Work said he took a personal day."

"Well that's nonsense, he isn't home."

"Where else would he be?"

"Westmoreland State Park, maybe. He goes for walks along the beach there sometimes."

"It's November."

"Maynard's ways are unusual. He's a very intelligent man and intelligent men are often difficult to understand for men such as yourself, Mr. Cogbill. Now if you'll please excuse me, I have a garden club meeting in half an hour."

The door slammed shut in my face.

I went east on Eden until I hit 301 near Alto, across from the building that had once been Vee Clare's Red Top Grill next to the black school, Ralph Bunche, and crossed the highway to

Hanover Church Road and out to 205. East of 301 it always felt as if I were leaving the modern world and disappearing into the grey fog of history, where the dead walked, restless to speak the truths they had taken to the grave, tales of loss and injustice inflicted upon them because of their station or the color of their skin. To charge us that we might yet build a world free of these calamities. But the living would not hear the dead and confronted by them would flee; and so the world would carry on much as it always had, in suffering and inequity, and finally to ash and dust.

The cold and mist of the early morning persisted as the long, narrow two-lane led me through field and forest, and murky swampland. I turned south onto Longfield Road just beyond Ninde, and dropped back out onto 205 at Reno Skypark, lately fallen into disuse.

Route 205 rejoined Route 3 in Oak Grove. A large school in sort of a modest Queen Anne style sat nearby, with two chimneys and a row of five dormers protruding from the green tin roof. It seemed to sort of sulk there in the mist, the yard awash in brown leaves, the black bones of the sleeping forest swaying gently behind.

I found the car right where Mrs. Carter said, out at Westmoreland State Park, down in the lot by the waterfront. Maynard was nowhere around. The Potomac looked like obsidian flecked with ash under the pale grey sky. Small, timid waves rolled in, carrying brown garlands of seaweed. The riverbank glistened with pebbles and colorful shell fragments, strewn with twisted black shapes of driftwood. There were fresh footprints, so I followed them among the flotsam, east along the shore. It was chilly and I pulled my mackinaw tighter around my neck, my hands thrust into my pockets, fedora pulled low. Here and there a tree had tumbled down from the cliff. After maybe a mile I found him sitting on a log, contemplating the river.

"Is that Maynard Carter?"

He looked up at me, in surprise.

"Er, Mr. Cogbill, isn't it? Strange weather for a walk on the beach."

"Well, I'm an intelligent man, Mr. Carter, and we're unusual in our ways."

He stared blankly at me.

"You okay?"

"Yes, Mr. Cogbill, I'm fine. I guess the untimely passing of a friend hits us all in unexpected ways."

"Yes it does."

"I'd like to be alone, if you don't mind."

"I spoke to Laura Dawson the other day."

"Who?"

"K Department secretary? Pretty blonde?"

"Is she? I hadn't noticed."

"Hard not to," I said.

"I'm married."

"Well, the thing is, she seemed to be pretty familiar with Dane. With his personal life."

His eyes flicked up towards me from the darkened recesses of his skull, and then snapped back to the water. Maryland was out there, somewhere. Cobb Island, Colton's Point. Invisible in the mist that hung over the cold, grey river.

"Is that so?"

"She said he had a difficult childhood. Never felt like he fit in. Sort of intimidated by other men."

He nodded. His hair fluttered and waved in the breeze off the river, for he wore no hat, and his cheeks were flushed pink with the cold.

"I suppose that's an accurate accounting, yes."

His coat was plain blue, sort of a work coat, and his shirt-tail hung below it, though the striped half-Windsor of a necktie was visible at his throat. His ill-fitting trousers, an awful brown, were so long or worn so low on his hips that they nearly reached the heels of his shoes though he was sitting down. There was evident wear at the hems. Probably he trod on them regularly.

"Did Dane and Miss Dawson spend much time together?"

"No. Well. Kind of, yes."

"Why didn't you mention this before, Maynard?"

"Just protecting Dane, I suppose. He was my best friend."

He smiled nervously, and I nodded.

"Did he need protecting?"

"I don't know. There are some things we don't, ah... I mean... you know. Even friends have secrets."

"Do you think Dane was having an affair?"

"I-I, I don't...pay attention to people. You understand? People are, ridiculous. They don't do things that, that make sense. There's no logic. Numbers make sense. Wiring makes sense, I can fix a radio or a flashlight or something, a little solder, a little twist of some copper. There's logic. My wife hates balancing the checkbook. I do it for fun. Hu-hu-human things, feelings, people going for walks and having conversations that stop when you walk in the room, it's like, I notice it, but it's tiresome, Mr. Cogbill. I don't concern myself with it.

"Numbers don't disappoint me. They are what they are. The, the solution to a math problem is an inevitability. The only inevitability with people is that there will be problems. Problems with no logical solution. So was Dane having an affair? If I'm being honest, probably so. But it's messy and I can't...deal with it, okay? And I go in that building, and he's not there, and the others are there, and conversations still stop when I walk in the room, and I, I feel things, Mr. Cogbill, but I can't work out the math to solve those feelings. I, I can't work out the math."

I left him there, sitting on the log. I felt bad that I'd dimed him to his wife. I hoped he wouldn't get in trouble. In hindsight she hadn't seemed particularly concerned that he might not be at work. She seemed to just take it for granted that he wasn't like other people. For sure Maynard Carter was a strange man; but I'd finally seen his humanity and the overwhelming feeling I had was pity. Maybe I also understood Dane Harris a little better as a result. Maybe Laura Dawson had given Dane a sense of belonging or acceptance that he hadn't felt before. Maynard was right: human problems are messy and have no neat, inevitable solutions.

The next afternoon, I pulled up to Salem Baptist Church in Welcome, with its crowned belfry, almost to Nanzatico. I had just come from work. My feet were sore and the skin on my hands resembled a lizard's ass, but Veola Clare had arranged that I should meet someone here. Outside was a rusty '43 Chevy coupe in powder blue, and a '48 Dodge 100 pickup in forest green. The pickup was waxed and the whitewalls and running boards were scrubbed free of dirt.

Inside, the sanctuary was wainscoted, and although it was small, there were balconies and three narrow rows of pews, one row under each balcony and one in the middle. Front and center, behind the altar, was the pulpit, and behind that a choir loft. Two black men stood near the altar and watched me enter. One,

IN THE TRACKLESS WILD | 143

an older man in a suit and tie, turned out to be the pastor. The other was the man I'd come to meet, Marion Washington.

Washington was tall and lanky, with dark skin and a pencil-thin moustache. His hair was mown close to the scalp, and although he was in his shirt-sleeves his clothes were coordinated and he was wearing cologne. He eyed me carefully, and didn't smile.

"Ronymus Cogbill?"

"Yes sir. Harry, please. Are you Mr. Washington?"

"That's right." He nodded curtly as he said it, and raised his eyebrows.

"Vee Clare said you were willing to talk to me."

"I ain't agreed to say a damn thing. I agreed to meet wit' you."

"Yes sir. Your mother used to work for him?"

"He say you know 'Lijah Taylor."

"Mr. Taylor is a friend of mine, yes sir."

"Where from?"

"I knew his son in the war."

"Bet."

"He died saving my life."

"That what niggas is worth to you?"

"He was my brother, Marion."

I felt my face doing things beyond my control, and I couldn't hold his gaze.

I flashed on a vision of myself, years ago in Belgium, after Ardennes, staring down a lieutenant named Carlisle.

"What's the matter, Cogbill? You're not still sore about that Taylor boy?"

I turned away from Carlisle and ripped the steel pot from my head.

"Hell, that's what niggers are for," he sang after me.

I wheeled on him, stepped up, still carrying that momentum, and swung the pot from my hip. I can still remember the sound when it connected with his jaw.

I came back to the present, standing in the church, Marion Washington looking at me strangely.

"Rollie my cousin."

"He was a brave man."

We both stood there a minute, not saying anything. The sanctuary grew brighter and then dimmer again as the sun briefly flirted with making an appearance.

"I'on't know where William be stayin' at. Get that out your mind."

"I don't need to know. Mainly I need to know he's safe."

"Safe last I seen 'im."

"Unless that was today, it doesn't count."

"What you know?"

"I think he's with a little Italian guy named Joey DeLarosa. And there's a mob enforcer named Feeley after DeLarosa. William's my friend, I don't want him getting caught in the middle."

Washington's eyebrows went up. "The brother's already in the middle."

"Can you get the message to William, about Feeley? He's a hunter, a crooked cop from Florida. A real psychopath."

"Bet."

"I think he works for a man named Adagio. Adagio's connected to Tom Boone."

"What you know about Tom Boone?"

"I know he's trash. And I know he's Micah Johnson's landlord. I know whatever William might have done was under duress."

Washington's manner seemed to soften a little.

"You want to help William, talk to them out the Beach. They know Boone."

"Who?"

"E'rebody."

"I'll ask around. Just make sure William's okay."

"Don't give me no orders."

I held my hands up, palms toward him, and let my face go slack.

"If William's with Joey, I know where they were last night. They left in a hurry this morning and I think Feeley might have found them too. I just don't know if he got there before or after they left. Joey DeLarosa's a lightning rod for bad luck."

Leaving Salem Church, I followed the road around and picked up Route 3 by Parker's Store in Index, and followed it to Oak Grove, with its green-roofed school, onto 205 toward the beach, past the end of the little defunct airstrip and the ghost of Monroe's birthplace, straight through Beachgate and into the town of Colonial Beach proper. The chimneys and hipped roof of Colonial Beach School rose up to the right, above the houses and the railroad diner, presiding over the little town. Ahead on a rise was the hotel, built around a mansion that had once been the summer home of Light-Horse Harry Lee. There was a small amusement park, shut down for the season, and beyond it, built on a huge pier out over the Potomac River, a once-famous night spot.

The river was technically within the state of Maryland; the shore, Virginia. Until a few years ago, Maryland state law had permitted gambling on piers, and as a result certain men with an eye for opportunity had turned Colonial Beach into a popular party destination. But the state government did what it has always done, namely screwing Virginians out of success in an effort to appease the pearl-clutchers, and made an arrangement that saw Maryland changing its laws. Now the businessmen who had made their living selling a good time to people in search of one, were struggling to keep themselves afloat.

I parked in a gravel lot and walked up a wide pier, over the state line to the club entrance under a large, red neon sign. Inside, rows of counters still sat empty where slot machines had once stood in rows like good little soldiers in the wide, low-ceilinged hall. The pinball machines under the plate glass windows shimmered and buzzed, but only one young man stood hunched over one of the games. The owner was a burly fellow with curly dark hair, apple-cheeks and a skinny necktie. His suit was tailored but no longer fit properly. He reminded me of a prizefighter doing a presser after losing the title. He was sitting at the horseshoe bar in the near-deserted club.

He watched me approach him and had the bartender get me a drink.

"Just a Coke," I said, although I didn't really want anything. His shoulders slumped a little when I said it. I guess selling Cokes wasn't going to keep him afloat.

"You the owner?"

"Oh boy, that depends who's asking."

"My name's Harry Cogbill. I wondered if we could talk about Tom Boone."

He rubbed his eyes with the heels of his hands and then slid them up over his head, smoothing his hair back.

"Tell that son of a bitch if he wants me to pay him anytime soon, to send a better class of heavy. Alright? Maybe somebody who'll spend a couple damn dollars on a glass of bourbon.

Fuckin' buzzards are circling and everybody walking by just wants to see a little blood."

His face had colored and I wondered about his blood pressure.

"I'm not from Boone," I said. "And I share your estimation of his character. I'm genuinely just looking for information."

"Yeah?" He exhaled so deeply I thought his ghost had tried to make a break for it. "Then forget everything I said, will ya? Especially the part where it might've sounded like I know him."

"How much are you into him for?"

"It's not like that. He was an investor, when I built all this."

"And now?"

"Look, the gambling was legal, right?"

"Technically, yeah."

"I used to give back to the community. I'm a law-abiding citizen here. Why I'm sinking in all this." He waved a hand at the wreck of his life. "Tommy? He found other ways to profit."

"Things that weren't so legal?"

"Exactly. Hell, it's sort of his fault the state shut us down. Only I'm losing my shirt and he's living in a mansion."

"Drugs or girls?"

"Boone? Both. This town was wild in the fifties."

"I've heard."

"I used to fly people in from Washington or Richmond. Congressmen, diplomats, lobbyists. Or drive them to the marina in Newburg and bring 'em right up to the pier. I could give them drinks, gambling, live music. Dancing. I mean that's classy, right? But some of those people really ain't all that classy."

"Did you know what was going on?"

"Well, not at first. But those powerful Washington types? I mean who'm I supposed to call? Besides, Colonial Beach police

148 I SEAN GATES

got no jurisdiction in here. Charles County Sheriffs got a long way to drive. Them power-players woulda shut me down in a couple minutes. Best just to look the other way."

"Did you see the stabbing? George Siever?"

"Out the old steamboat pier? No, I was here."

"Do you know William Johnson?"

He looked down and rose from his stool. "I got work to do."

"Yeah, this place is really hopping."

He started away, into the desolation of the club.

"Enjoy your Coke." He didn't turn back when he said it.

I tipped the bartender and left the soft drink untouched.

CHAPTER TWELVE

MR. CLARE had closed the Circle Supermarket for Thanksgiving. He sent me home with a turkey that I wasn't sure what Ethel and I would even do with, considering it would be just the two of us for dinner. So I got some potatoes and a can of cranberry jelly. I am not always fancy. On Thursday I got up early, started the coffee, and dressed the turkey while the oven preheated.

Fawkes wandered into the kitchen and sat watching my every move. He winked sleepily, yawned, and smacked his lips. He could pretend he wasn't interested, but I knew better. Once the turkey was in the oven, I got out my skillet and put on some bacon. I got down a cereal bowl, cracked four eggs, added a splash of milk, a dash of crushed red pepper, and whipped the whole thing with a fork until it was smooth and yellow, and fried it in some butter. I made toast and got out the jelly, and in a little while Ethel appeared.

It was a cold morning and her robe was cinched tightly at her waist. I poured her a cup of coffee and she sort of hunched over it as she took her first tentative sip. Fawkes dashed over to her and sort of circled her a few times.

"Mornin', Guy."

He made happy little fox sounds, sort of a raspy whine, and squinted up at her. I plated up the eggs, bacon, and toast, and put down a bowl of Purina for Fawkes, hoping to distract him.

"Hieronymus I still don't see why you couldn't invite Elijah and Iris for dinner."

"They didn't come to the barbecue. We've been trying for over a year."

"So we keep trying. Sooner or later they're bound to say yes."

"I don't want to pressure them. Besides, Frank may show up."

Ethel pushed her eggs around the plate a little.

"We both know he won't."

I shouldn't have mentioned it. Ethel had invited him, as she always did to our parties and dinners and events.

"It's just so frustratin', Cogbill."

"I know." I wanted to say it was my fault, that I was a pariah, a leper, and always had been. She shouldn't have married me.

"Well you an' me and Fawkes are gonna have the best damn Thanksgiving anybody ever had, and that's just the end of it."

After breakfast I did the dishes, and while Ethel was in the shower I drove over to her daddy's place. I didn't have a plan. The prickly, khaki fields were scattered with leaves the color of old pennies, the once carefully maintained barbed wire fences wrapped with strands of sleeping grapevine and thorny snarls of wild blackberry.

The old Aermotor whined plaintively as it spun drowsily atop its tower. I parked in the muddy loop and clambered up on the porch; I had to skip the step because it had broken. The porch sagged and creaked under my weight. I pounded on the door.

"Frank. Open up, Frank! We need to talk."

His face appeared, less man than ghoul, in the narrow, six-inch strip of darkness where he pulled the door open.

"What do you want?"

"Come over for dinner, Frank. It's Thanksgiving."

"Don't want to."

"I can't stand to see her this upset. You understand that, don't you? We have plenty of food. We want you to come."

"She don't want me there. Hates me."

"You're her father, Frank."

The face disappeared from the aperture. I heard some shuffling and creaking of floorboards inside. There was a crash.

"Frank? You okay?"

"Goddammit. Stupid damn house..."

"Frank?"

"Stupid damn..."

I pushed the door open, gently. Frank was in a strap undershirt and pajama pants, a robe with no sash. His hair would have made me laugh if the circumstances were different. The house stank. It was evident he hadn't cleaned anything in a while. He was on his ass in the middle of the floor.

"Frank." I went to help him up and he pushed me away violently.

"Goddammit don't touch me."

"Frank are you drunk?"

"Get out. Leave. Go home."

"Aw, Frank."

"I'm fine. Get out."

I extended my hand, and did not leave.

He glared at me. I kept my face expressionless.

"Are you sure you're not hurt?"

"I'm not that damned old."

"Then take my damn hand, Frank."

I saw his resolve wavering. Finally he took my hand and I pulled him up.

"I'll make you some coffee."

He didn't say anything, which felt enough like progress that I braved the kitchen. Now I've worked in a number of commercial kitchens, and I have seen some things no diner wants to know about, but I can only describe Frank Burkitt's kitchen as having been absolutely defiled. If it had been summer, there'd have been an infestation.

I scrubbed out the percolator and searched the cabinets for a can of grounds. There was a dented can of Chock Full O' Nuts in the pantry. All around the kitchen I could see signs of Alice Pope Burkitt. The tea curtains on the window over the sink, a cheerful yellow with strawberries and little white flowers on them. The plates in the sink, many chipped, that she had definitely chosen, blue and white, delicate and dainty. The linen tea towel in a heap on the counter, once soaked through, now stiffened into its present shape, printed with a picture of a basket of tomatoes.

While the percolator gasped and burbled, I washed the dishes and straightened up what I could. I wondered where Frank was, and if I should check on him, but he hadn't kicked me out or shot me to death, and I was content to take the W. I poured Frank a cup and carried it into the living room.

"What's your angle, Cogbill?"

"You're her father, Frank."

I put the coffee on the side table. He looked at it, and then at me.

"What time's dinner?"

"Say two-thirty?"

"Two-thirty."

"But you can come early. Hell, if you want I'll wait while you get cleaned up and you can ride with me..."

"You'd like that. Be the hero."

"I just want to see her smile."

"Yeah." He nodded. Maybe it had finally occurred to him we had that in common.

I left him there and went home to make green beans and mashed potatoes. Ethel was reading a book by Thomas Lomax Hunter, and Fawkes was prowling around the house sniffing the air, I assume wondering when the turkey would be ready.

"Well there you are! Where'd you go, Cogbill?"

"Had to run an errand."

"Pretty sure ever'thin's closed."

"Seems that way."

"What'd you, go to invite the Taylors?"

"I don't want to get your hopes up."

She put the book down and looked at me.

"We're enough, Harry Cogbill. You and me and Guy."

She was right. Inside the house was everything I needed or wanted. I sat down beside her and took her in my arms, and I could smell her musky scent, and her strawberry-scented hair and feel her warmth and the steady rise and fall of her breathing, and considered not for the first time nor the last, that I was indeed thankful.

"We need to finish making dinner, Harry Cogbill."

"Probably."

"What if company comes?"

"I don't know that they will."

"Might do."

"I don't want to get your hopes up."

"Well if they don't we'll still be thankful, and we can show each other just how much. After dinner."

"Yes ma'am."

"Now how many places should I set?"

"Probably two."

"With room for more."

"Always room for more."

Later, with the beans and the mashed potatoes on low and the smell of the turkey permeating our little house, I looked out the window across the misty fields, the forest a vague silver wall in the distance, and watched a ragged line of poor farmers and children in mismatched uniforms of grey and beige wool marching toward Fredericksburg. It is often difficult for Americans from the North to understand that we southerners live in twice-conquered land. For the Europeans took it from the Indians and then the north conquered the south, and many things both good and bad have been lost in the fog of war. The effect that has on a people isn't something that most Americans will ever stop to consider. I suspect in Europe they would understand it more fully.

Ethel put Fawkes in his pen while I plated up the food. We had just sat down to eat when there was a knock at the door, and I stood in the hall as Ethel opened the door to see her father, clean and shaven, hair combed back, standing on our porch. He held a fedora in his hands and turned it nervously by the brim in shaky fingers.

"Sorry I'm late, babygirl. The house's kind of a mess."

"Daddy?"

"Cogbill invited me. If y'don't want me here I unnerstand, I been kind of—"

"Daddy!" She threw her arms around him and he hugged her and I saw his eyes glisten, but he made no acknowledgement of it and would not meet my eye.

I put down a third place-setting and cut him a good-sized piece of turkey breast, gave him a heap of potatoes and a healthy pile of beans and a big hunk of cranberry jelly, and with the ladle I put a neat crater in the center of the potato mound and filled it with gravy, and placed the whole thing in front of him, with a mug of coffee and a glass of water.

I'd like to tell you that all our problems disappeared the moment Frank Burkitt knocked on our door and came into our home for the first time. For a moment I even believed it would go that way. But that's a child's view of the world, the stuff of Hollywood, the happy finish to a Jimmy Stewart picture. And that has never been my world.

"It smells delicious, Ethel."

"Was Cogbill made it."

Frank didn't say anything, but tucked his napkin into his shirt-collar.

"Does it ever wake you at night, Cogbill? Knowing that you shot an innocent kid in the street?"

"Daddy Franklin Burkitt, that is no way to talk to your host."

"Yes, Frank."

"Hieronymus? That really happened?"

"In Europe. Yes."

"Why didn't you tell me?"

"I told you I had seen and done things I wouldn't want to taint your imagination with."

"Well it was a war..."

"I panicked. I shouldn't have shot."

"And then you let that colored boy die for you."

"Rollie Taylor. His name was Rollie Taylor."

"You couldn't even shoot your gun. How you think you're gonna defend my daughter if anybody comes here looking for trouble?"

"I can handle myself, Daddy!"

"You shouldn't have to, babygirl."

"He's right, Ethel."

Frank looked at me, his face unreadable.

"He's right. You had to shoot Nestor Lazos because I wasn't here. Even if I was here, I might have frozen. If you were counting on me, you might have died."

"We're a team, Hieronymus. We have each other's back. Daddy, I believe I'd like you to leave now."

"No." Nobody was more surprised than I was to hear the word coming out of my mouth. "No. Let's get this out in the open. Frank, since you know so much about my military career, how about I tell you the way it happened? You too, Ethel. Stick around, maybe it's for the best."

It was dusk. This was before Rollie and I were in the same unit, before Ardennes. It was a little village in Belgium. It was half blown to hell, and we limped in after getting cut to ribbons by German artillery in the hills. Half of our unit was wounded or killed. The ones the medics could strap back together, we dragged into town on biers we'd made from tents or slickers, and whatever sticks we could come up with. Even the sunset looked like blood-soaked rags.

The lieutenant was a man named Carlisle. Like a lot of officers he figured he was smarter than everybody else and he let us know it often. It was his fault we blundered into that line of artillery, but I never heard him own his responsibility. He blamed it on others. He was a coward and the dead couldn't talk back.

I think we were all a little paranoid, creeping into that village. I expected a sniper on every rooftop, in the belfry of the little church on the edge of town. But for a long time, nothing came. It might have been five or ten minutes, it felt like hours. Near the crossroads at the center of town, the road was blocked by a heap of brick and stone. A bakery with a residence above it, the front of the building just...gone. I guess we were picking our way over it in the street.

Inside you could see pipes, and furniture all covered in dust. Towels abandoned where they hung on a rack. A three-legged dog, hunched and emaciated, shied from us and disappeared down an alley. There were toys in the street, tools. A lady's Sunday hat. All at once there was a shout and movement out of the corner of my eye. I didn't see, I didn't think. It was instinct. I was looking for trouble, I was sure there was a whole platoon of Nazis somewhere waiting to finish the job their big guns had started. I just shot.

"You didn't know, Hieronymus."

"It's not like in the movies. He didn't fall backwards. He was running to us, looking for help. His momentum carried him forward. He just sprawled facedown and didn't move. I realized too late. His mother ran out into the street and threw herself on top of him, crying. Cursing us. I can still remember the sound of her screams. Carlisle shot her. In the head. To shut her up. And that was my fault too. Because if I hadn't shot the kid, he wouldn't have had to shoot her. That's the way he explained it to me. So. Yeah."

I looked Frank Burkitt dead in the eye and waited for him to speak. He didn't.

"Sometimes at night when I'm about to fall asleep, I can still see that place, and the boy and his mother are there, in the street, looking at me. In judgment. And I don't blame them."

Ethel reached over and took my hand. She was looking at me with wide eyes. "You could have told me. It ain't your fault. Carlisle's responsible for his own actions, Cogbill. And I'm responsible for mine. It ain't your fault I had to shoot Nestor. It's Nestor's."

"Frank's right, though. I had trouble pulling the trigger after that. Maybe if I didn't, Rollie Taylor would still be alive. He was the best guy I've ever known. It's my fault he's dead, and I've had to live with that every day for sixteen years."

Ethel squeezed my hand and looked at me with patient understanding. Frank took a drink of water. There were beads of sweat on his forehead. His face was nearly purple; he looked around the room as though in search of something he'd misplaced, then took the napkin from his collar, stood up, and started toward the front door. He looked briefly in confusion at his left arm, turned to say something, gasping for air.

"Daddy? Daddy!"

I stood up. "Ethel get the car keys. Get the car keys!"

She gathered herself and did exactly that while I helped Frank to my car, and the three of us drove for Fredericksburg as fast as the Pontiac would go. We were just across the Stafford County line when Frank finally spoke.

"I feel better now."

"Daddy you're going to the hospital and I won't hear anything more about it."

"It's Thanksgiving."

"You had a heart attack, Frank."

"Was indigestion."

"Oh bullshit, daddy."

She said it softly, almost tenderly, and would not let go of him.

Frank was going to make it, not such a surprise given that he was awake and alert when we pulled up to the aging, two-story Mary Washington Hospital at the corner of Sophia and Fauquier. They kept him for observation.

Evidently Reverend Shomo paid him a visit the next day.

"You hadn't been taking care of yourself, Frank."

"I got a lot on my mind."

"Sure that's so. Life's full of challenges."

"I'm tired, reverend."

"I could come back another time."

"I'm tired of life."

The remark hung there, like the sagging roof of an old barn.

"Why are you tired of life, Frank?"

"It ain't that I want to die or nothing, I just..."

The pastor waited, perhaps mentally searching the scriptures for something useful to say. Shomo was about sixty-seven, and had a large family, and Frank for his part was unsure that the reverend could understand.

"The house is so damned empty, preacher."

"Yes, Musean and I felt that way when the last of our girls moved out. It's not unusual."

"But it's full, too."

The preacher inclined his head.

"In what way, Frank?"

"The furniture, the drapes, the goddamned plates, begging your pardon reverend...Alice picked them out. The dish-towels, the bath towels, everything. She's everywhere I look."

"Well of course she is. She was your wife."

"And then Ethel goes and marries that son of a bitch and leaves me behind with all of that, that shit I bought her momma, and I can't touch nothing in there without thinking of her, Arta. Nothing."

"I hear you, Frank. What I have to say isn't going to be easy for you, but I think you need to hear it. Will you listen?"

"Well where in Christ's name am I gonna go?"

Shomo let the remark pass.

"It sounds to me like you made Ethel responsible for your happiness."

"You son of a bitch, get out."

"Aw, I didn't mean it that way, Frank. I'm saying your grief is your responsibility. I'm saying you have to let Alice go, or you'll never heal. I'm saying God wants you to let Him in."

Shomo left him there in the hospital bed, defeated, to face what St. John of the Cross called the dark night of the soul. Whatever happened next, Frank never spoke of. But I know of my own experience that when you've sunk as far you can go, and wallowed, and railed against the Lord on His throne, eventually, like a child in a tantrum, you exhaust yourself. Your eyes open and you see where you are and what you've become, and you get up, and you breathe. And you climb.

CHAPTER THIRTEEN

MARION WASHINGTON shined his shoes, changed his shirt, rubbed oil into his coarse, crew-cut curls and ran a comb over them. He shaved and shaped up the pencil-thin moustache, put on aftershave, and drove his gleaming green Dodge out the dirt road to Jersey and then to highway 301, where a few plain cinderblock buildings slouched off the shoulder in a gravel lot between a wood and a few small houses. A barn light was screwed into a red oak and cast a blue-white glow across the gravel. Boogie-woogie was cranking from a speaker inside the building.

There was a ragged row of humpbacked sedans all at least a decade old, and a circle of black men whose raised voices were raucous in the country night as they catcalled after a young woman named Charise, whose breasts and buttocks swelled dramatically against her simple cotton dress, and whose full lips gleamed purple under the barn light.

"Baby gotDAMN!"

"Is yo' mans home?"

"My mans ain't none a your bidness," she said.

"An' I sho ain't none a his!"

The men howled as Charice disappeared into the rectangle of yellow light in front of the cinderblock building. One of the men, a rangy guy in a porkpie hat with a complexion like black silk, came over and touched the hood of Marion's truck.

"Gotdamn, brother, is it any wax LEFT?"

"Finger my shit again, nigga, I'mma wax yo ass."

"I ain't trynna start nothing, nigga. Be cool, brotha, be cool."

Marion pursed his lips and lifted his eyebrows. "Bet."

Inside they were selling barbecue and collard greens, and bottles of beer out of a cooler and something harder that may or may not have been legally distilled.

The cinderblock walls were slathered with a thick coat of paint that was scratched with initials and other cryptic messages, and peeling around the window and door. The floor was sawdust, the counter was plywood and the few tables were mismatched and so were most of the chairs. Charise was sitting at the counter. Behind the counter a large woman in an apron wiped her hands on a rag and smiled at Washington.

"Well hey there, M. Brotha lookin' SHARP."

"Smell like heaven up in here, 'Nita."

"Course it do, you see me cookin', ain't you?"

He smiled at her and feigned indignation. Then he turned to Charise.

"Them niggas outside ain't give you a bad time, did they?"

"I just go wit' it, M. They ain't mean no harm."

Marion drew his mouth into a line and opted not to reply.

Arnita put a drink in front of Marion and made a show of holding out a hand until he slipped a bill into it. Some old men were playing cards in the corner, gossiping and swapping dirty jokes. After a while Arnita slid a plate of barbecue in front of Washington and pressed her knuckles into her hips.

"Now if you ain't come out wit' what it is you want to ax..."

Marion's eyebrows shot up and his face split in a broad smile.

"How you know I wanna ax something?"

"Cos it's written all over your face, honey."

"An' you cain't help lookin' at my face."

"A fine dark brotha like you come strutting in my door, I'mma look real long and real hard."

"Now you just looking for a good tip."

"Depends what tip you talkin' bout."

"Oh, Lord..." His voice rose in feigned shock.

Arnita laughed. "So what you wanna ax, honey?"

Marion looked around the room again. The old men in the corner weren't paying attention. The music was loud enough to cover the conversation if he kept his voice low.

"I'm looking for a brother owes me money."

"Bet."

"Reverend said he might be here."

"He might. Lot of brothers pass through here."

"I got some news he might want."

"Reverend done told me. Stick around after we close up."

It was late when Arnita pushed the last of the patrons out and locked the door. She led Marion out the back of the one-room building and across the yard where a separate kitchen stood, another simple concrete building with a chimney and a door, and couple of high windows like a bunker that shone with yellow light.

"He was hiding out at the church for a while," Marion said.

"He said that. He also say you done kicked him out. Deacon."

"He left to go help a friend."

"A friend?"

"Some New York Italian."

Inside was a big man who was not William Johnson. He looked up as they entered, sized up Marion Washington, and looked to Arnita. His face was round and sort of flat, and he was missing several teeth.

"He the one reverend said about," she offered the cook by way of explanation.

The old grist mill was down a forested dirt track, a brooding, hunched-over silhouette against the ragged strip of night sky over the silvered ribbon of the creek. The wheel sat immobile, the windows like darkened eye sockets in the weathered timber face. Parked nearby was a battered green Chevy with a busted window, missing its hood insignia. The big cook, whose name was Johnny Davis, had driven Marion out to the mill. Now he took a paper sack from the trunk of his old Ford and thrust it into Marion's hands.

Davis lit an old gas-powered railroad lantern as he led Marion up the stone steps and onto the millstone floor. The ceiling was low and the yellow light from the lantern threw shadows from the timber beams and the cobwebby tun, chute, and millstones. There were axels and pinions crisscrossing the room, some of which had fallen. In back a set of darkened, narrow stairs went down into a dank cellar full of heavy cogs and dry-rotted belts.

A crouched shadow moved among the cog wheels, just for an instant.

"Johnny?"

"Yeh. Come on out William."

When he stepped into the pool of yellow light, Johnson's clothes were dirty, his hair was bushy and unkempt, and he'd grown a beard.

"Marion?"

"Hey brother." He gave William the paper sack.

"Clean threads," Johnny said.

"Thanks."

"It's a white man asking 'bout you," Marion said. "Name of Cogbill."

"I know him."

"You trust him?"

"Ain't sure now."

"I ain't tell him nothing."

"He might could've helped Mr. Joey, but he ain't."

"What happened?"

"I's gathering firewood. Hunter got him."

"Hunter?"

"Kind that hunt men."

"Cogbill said about him. He a bent cop name of Feeley. Might be connected to Boone."

"So he prob'ly after me too."

"What about your sister?"

"I don't know, man. I got nobody turn to."

"You cain't live in no rickety fucking mill forever neither. Sooner or later the cops find you."

"Or the hunter."

"That Joey's car outside?"

"Yeah."

"I leave it in a parking lot somewhere. Johnny follow me, take me back to my truck."

"Your black ass get pulled over, best believe I keep right on driving, too."

Marion's eyebrows shot up and he blinked a couple times, gave a rapidly repeating nod. "A'ight, bet."

Marion's bowels felt watery and his arms and neck frozen as he drove Joey DeLarosa's car through a sleeping King George County. The green Bel Air needed a new muffler and the motor was tapping. One of the headlights was busted where William had hit a deer speeding away after Feeley had carried off Joey's body in the trunk of his car. Even in the dark the Chevy was conspicuous, and although the headlights of Johnny Davis's Ford were all that was visible in the rearview, Marion kept expecting to see Sheriff Powell or one of the enthusiastic State Troopers eating up the road behind him.

But apart from a couple of tractor-trailers and late-night travelers, 301 was deserted. The first place he came to that suited him was the motor court at Edgehill. The neon sign was turned off and although there were several cars parked in the paved lot between the three buildings, there were no lights on. He turned off the headlights and parked nose-in on the left-hand side. He quickly wiped down the surfaces with his handkerchief and left the car in the lot. He crossed the grass to a small filling station next door, jumped into Davis's waiting Ford and rode back to the little cluster of cinderblock buildings where his pickup was waiting alone in the field, the dampened barn light in the red oak humming faintly, the silver moon reflecting off the pristine wax finish.

About an hour after dawn, Eamon Feeley stepped out of his room in the Edgehill Motel and down the narrow concrete steps from the sidewalk to the paved lot. The two lodges were faced in stone and had lean-to roofs that slanted backward from the lot. They were plain, even rather ugly, but a modern neon sign stood on a post beside a utility pole. The third building, the office, stood at the back end of the lot, closing the narrow U. It sat on a rise and the land was tiered in several steps up to the entrance. It had a stone chimney rising from a shallow pyramid roof in the center, and a red brick chimney at each end.

Feeley had a cigarette dangling from his mouth as he tugged on the new hunting jacket he'd picked up from a little sporting goods store at Carruther's Corner a few miles out 205. He couldn't see any reason for the name; apart from the little store the corner had nothing much to recommend it. Feeley was thinking about breakfast until his eyes lit on the green Chevy brooding halfway up the sad little lot. The last time he'd seen it, it was crouching behind the ruins where he'd caught up with Joey Delarosa. Someone was sending him a message. They knew what he'd done.

An elderly couple came out from one of the rooms with their bags in tow as Feeley slowly circled the Chevy.

"That your car, mister? I think some negroes took it for a joyride last night. I woke up to go to the bathroom and saw the headlights come in. I saw him park it here, jump out and run away."

Breakfast would wait. He got in his Lincoln and sped down 301 to Office Hall although he did not know the name, for the large house on the corner with its abandoned summer kitchen and servants' quarters meant nothing to him; and turned left onto Route 3 toward Shiloh. At Index he stopped at Parker's Store, a two-story clapboard affair with a gallery porch and counters down both sides of the interior, with stairs at the back winding their way up to a second-level catwalk. The morning sun made dust motes in the rafters far above his head, and the hardwood creaked as he picked out a Coca-Cola and a Moon Pie and paid for his gas.

He felt that he had stepped into the old west, or the small town from some TV comedy where the drunk let himself into the jail every afternoon. He had lived in Boston, and in Palm Beach, and had served in the Navy on destroyers in the Pacific. He was used to structure. To regiment. Rule of law. He knew how to flout it, and how to use it for his own protection. Like the night he'd thrown that sniveling kid off the foc's'le of the Gearing-class can he'd started on doing maintenance detail. They'd put the kid in charge, an Ensign fresh out of Annapolis, and he had his sights on his railroad tracks and was always barking up everybody's ass. So one night smoking a cigarette the kid goes missing and was never seen again. No witnesses. It was presumed he fell overboard or jumped. But Eamon Feeley knew.

This place was like that. A community isolated from the rest of the world, thinking they were civilized. Anything could happen here. The swamps weren't like the ones he hunted in back home – there was a marked absence of giant, ravenous lizards – but they weren't so different in spirit. He added a coil of rope to the meager pile on the counter and slid a few bills to the man behind the big brass register.

The rope went in his trunk. The Moon Pie and the Coke, he swallowed in a rush, belched voluminously, and threw the packaging out the window as he arced along Salem Church Road and found the narrow track by the landmark tree and the shotgun house, out to Nanzatico. A gaggle of honking, shitting geese took to the air from the stubbled fields.

He pulled into the looping drive among the ancient out-buildings of the plantation house. Just to the right of the circle was a small white clapboard building with a chimney protruding from a pyramid roof. There were a couple of vehicles parked nearby, and a man was standing in the bushes running a big movie camera on a tripod pointed in through one of the narrow windows of the little outbuilding. Feeley got out of the Lincoln. The door to the little building opened and Boone stepped out. Behind him, Feeley could see it was the old plantation's business office. A teenage girl wearing nothing but high heels and a nervous smile was flinging her discarded underthings across the room.

"That's right, honey, whatever you feel like doing," Boone said as he eased the door closed.

He was wearing his ridiculous shooting vest, and the shape of his johnson pressed out against his twill trousers.

"What the shit is this?"

"Well that's none of your concern, Feeley. It's business. Not the business you're here for."

"Some wiseass left that dago's car at my motel last night."

"Are you drunk?"

"The old lady said some darky dropped it there and ran off like he thinks he's the Shadow or something."

"Christ, man. How can anyone start a bottle this early?"

"I'm not drunk." Feeley threw his arm around Boone's shoulders and walked him away from the plantation office. "That girl in there is sixteen if she's a day, Tommyboy. Now I'm a man of taste myself, and I understand all the blood ain't in your brain right now, but I need you to listen to me, okay? Hector had me up here for to take out a punk dago who got a bunch of his paisanos shot to shit on a New York pier. I understand you got a little personnel problem yourself. A backwoods jigaboo who did a little wetwork for you and disappeared. I know you don't want him talking to nobody on the Job. I'm saying I think he's fucking with us. So how about you roll your big boy back up and start thinking with your other head, okay?"

Micah Johnson's house was across the rolling lawn beyond the summer kitchen to the left of the main house. It was an old slave quarters, about the size of a one-room schoolhouse, with a red tin roof, a small, covered porch, and open footings. It hunkered near the treeline out of view of the bay, and Feeley stood back as Boone knocked on the door.

"Micah, would you open up?"

"He will or I will."

Boone pounded harder.

"Now damn it, Micah, open up this instant!"

"It ain't no reason get angry, no sir. I's old an' I ain't moving too fast."

The door opened a crack and Micah's creased face appeared in the space, a glistening eye and a glint of teeth.

"My friend Mr. Feeley thinks your son might still be in town."

"I ain't know nothin' 'bout that, no sir. Ain't seen him since he done that thing out the beach."

"But you know who his friends are."

"Ain't my boy in trouble enough? Why would he truck wit' Mr. Feeley? Do he know you, sir?"

Feeley's Irish was coming up. It was like a plucked guitar string in his spine. His hands balled into fists and his face felt hot, the muscles in his big sloping shoulders bunching like rocks along a fault line. Boone spoke first.

"Now Micah, we're just talking here, is all. You know I want to help your family, I always have."

"Like you done he'p Esther?"

"I'm sure she's making good money in Baltimore."

"I know the truth, sir. I always knowed it. I know what she doing in Baltimore."

Boone's face turned ugly, but just for a second.

"No shame in using God-given talent, Micah."

"What you know 'bout God, or shame, sir?"

Feeley had heard enough. He leapt up onto the little porch, flung Boone aside like a scarecrow, and shouldered the door. Micah Johnson went sprawling and cracked his head on the plank floor. Feeley hoisted the old man onto his shoulder and carried him out of the house. Boone looked indignant but knew better than to chastise the big Irishman.

"Take him to the springhouse," he said instead. "Behind the summer kitchen."

Feeley didn't know what a summer kitchen was. The plantation was just a bunch of crummy old houses to him, sure they were pretty but buildings that old were rarely worth the effort. Like an old Model T that would have taken more time and money to keep up than just buying a new car. Pointless. He glared at Boone.

"Just follow the treeline," Boone said. "To the right. Here, come on."

Boone led him to a low, narrow building with no windows. It was nearly an A frame building, almost the only walls being the whitewashed gables front and back. A small plank door filled the height of the front gable. Boone unlocked it and Feeley tossed the old one-armed man inside and negotiated his bulk through the small opening. He stepped down into a shallow dugout space with clear water in a kind of trough bubbling in from somewhere underground.

Feeley threw Boone his car keys. "There's rope. In my trunk."

The ugly thing appeared in Boone's face again, but he only said "right," and shut the door behind him.

"Now that he's gone we can talk," Feeley said. "I'm gonna level with you. I'm a cop. I'm from Boston, originally, you know where that is? It's up north. Things are different up there."

"Don't be insulting me, sir."

"I can help your son. But I have to find him before the local boys do, you understand? If they catch him down here he'll never see the inside of a jail cell. You know it's true."

"You from Boston you ain't got no jurisdiction here."

"I got connections. I can get him far from here. Off the books."

"Mr. Boone say you think William still in town. Why you think that?"

"If he was here, who would he go to for help? Names and addresses. Before Boone gets back."

"What you gone do with the rope out your trunk, sir?"

"Well that's completely up to you."

And then the stiff old plank door pulled open and there was Boone, a coil of rope in one hand, the car keys in the other, his silhouette engraved against the blue silken sky.

CHAPTER FOURTEEN

LATER THAT MORNING I was doing the dishes and listening to Johnny Cash while Ethel played with Fawkes, and the sunlight streamed in through the back windows and caught dust motes swirling in the air above the chairs, and I thought that the world was a fine place and as full of wonders as it had seemed when I was a boy in Chester, running with my cousins around the yard at Magnolia Grange, and the Chesterfield County Sheriff, a tall gangly man with jug-handle ears and thick curly hair, whose round glasses and wide eyes below angling, bushy brows gave him the appearance of a very lean and learned owl, would light the woodstove in the Methodist Church near the courthouse on Sunday mornings.

There was a knock at the door and when I opened it, our own sheriff, Jay Powell, was standing on the porch with his octagonal hat in his hands and a grim look on his pie-plate face. His hair was slicked back neat as ever, but his little mouth was puckered and his broad, sloping shoulders heaved once and sort of sagged.

"Good morning, Jay."

"Well it's morning at least," he said.

"You want to come in? Cup of coffee maybe?"

"Reckon I could do with a cup about now, sure."

He stamped his feet on the mat before he stepped across the threshold.

"Well howdy miss Ethel."

"Howdy yerself, Sheriff. You've met Fawkes."

"I have encountered that wayward critter before, yes ma'am."

"Won't you sit down?"

"Much obliged."

I got the percolator going and set out an extra cup.

"You have sweet cream?"

"Jesus, Jay, what are you, some kind of Philistine?"

He didn't laugh, and Ethel shot me a look, so I decided to dial it down.

I got him a spoon and a saucer, a bowl of sugar and a bottle of milk out of the fridge. "You want this in a little decanter or anything? Maybe a doily to go under the saucer?"

"Gotdammit, Cogbill, I know you're playing but I'm really not in the mood."

The truth was, I had my suspicions about why he'd come, and I suppose I was trying to avoid it.

"Miss Ethel, you may want to leave the room, or Cogbill an' I can step out on the porch, this idn't somethin' you need to hear."

"Now Jay, I'm not a delicate li'l flower cain't handle grownup talk. I grew up on a farm. We been through this before."

He ran his hands over his face, smoothed his hair back.

"Awright, if that's the way you want it."

He added some milk and sugar to his coffee, then took out a flask and added something else. Took a sip.

"Not bad."

He added a little more from the flask before disappearing that vessel, and took another sip, savoring it. He sat back.

"We found your boy DeLarosa. Or a fisherman did, anyway. He were tangled up in the lines of a crab pot out by the Lower Cedar Point Beacon."

"In the Potomac?"

"That's right. The fisher ain't know who to call, but he's a King George feller so he called us. Had to work it out with the Navy and Charles County since they think they own the river."

"You're sure it's Joey?"

"Well, the crabs had been at him. It weren't pretty. But he had an old injury to one leg. Been dead a few days, probably. Who else is it gonna be?"

"You're not sure."

"Sure as I can be. Doc's trying to track down his dental records. They're working on it."

"He had a family."

"Where are they?"

"I don't know, he implied he sent them away."

Powell nodded.

"You know what I'm sick of, Cogbill? I mean really good and goddamn sick of? I'm sick of come-heres bringing all their baggage and their bullshit, pardon me Miss Ethel, and polluting my goddamn county. Begging your pardon again."

"For Heaven's sake, Sheriff."

"I'm just the messenger, Jay."

"I know, Cogbill."

"And the Indians who used to live here would probably say the same thing about our ancestors."

"Well they might've had a point."

I didn't disagree.

"I got no deputy, it's just me and a couple State Troopers think they're hot shit. That Johnson boy been at large for months. If he's smart he's nowhere near here. Broke his daddy's heart, Boone ain't seen him, or leastways says he hadn't. None of the nigras out there will talk to me. Hell I don't even blame 'em."

"Don't worry about William."

He looked at me, and I tried to keep my face neutral.

"Where'd Feeley say he was going, that day he barged into the restaurant?"

"The Vittorios' place. The Ernest Pie. Adagio's behind them too. Probably laundering money."

"One of them State boys found DeLarosa's car early this morning parked at the Edgehill Motel. Hood insignia missing, one headlight hanging out, a side window smashed in. Hoping we can get some kind of evidence out of it. Your boy Feeley is staying there. What do you make of that?"

"Why would Feeley leave Joey's car there?"

"Because when he takes a shit it fills up his skull and comes out his mouth. Who knows why crooks do what they do? They're damaged, Cogbill."

I wasn't so sure. Maybe it hadn't been Feeley who dumped the car there. Maybe it was a message. Maybe William was still alive.

Powell had finished his coffee. He stood, thanked us, apologized again for his language, which I knew Ethel found amusing, and I followed him to the door. When he got outside he put his hat on and turned to face me.

"You know what the worst part is?"

"What's that, Sheriff?"

"I like the goddamn pizza."

Later, Ethel and I drove over to John's store to pick up the mail, some dog food and a couple of other necessities. Then after dropping them off at the house, we went into town to visit Frank at Mary Washington.

"How're you feeling, daddy?"

"Fine. Better if they'd let me the hell out of here."

"They'll let you out when they decide you're ready."

"After they've laid to rest the last of my dignity," he said. "You see this, Cogbill? You see what I got to wear? He knows what I mean."

Frank? Talking to me? He didn't meet my eyes when he did it, and I admit I did wonder what was happening.

"Um, yeah I do." I tried to keep the question out of my voice but I don't believe I succeeded.

"Now daddy, it's only for a little while."

"I hope so."

"Did Mr. Shomo come see you?"

"Preacher come yesterday."

"What did he have to say?"

His eyes narrowed and he looked at a point somewhere to his left.

"Just the usual, you know. See how I's feeling. Say a prayer, put me on the list. I expect everyone at church'll be laughing about me tomorrow."

"Now daddy you know that's not true."

At last Frank turned his eyes to me, but just as quickly turned them away.

"Not too sure."

That evening Feeley pulled up to a concrete structure in a gravel lot under a barn light screwed into a red oak. The men in the parking lot sharing a laugh all stopped when they saw the Lincoln, and started to approach it in admiration. Until the big white man in the trilby got out, and then the silence was absolute.

"You ain't welcome here, cracker."

Feeley pulled his pistol and flashed a badge. The men disbursed, and some got in their vehicles. He went through the door and in a moment several old men staggered out without a word and drove away.

The woman behind the counter kept her face even as Feeley stared her down.

"You Arnita Lewis?"

"Who's askin'?"

"Me. I just asked. Are you Arnita Lewis?"

"There somethin' I can do for you?"

"Where's William Johnson?"

"I don't know nobody by that name, sir."

His big arm shot out and before she could react he had slapped her to the floor. When she opened her eyes he was crouched over her like a big bear, a pistol gripped in one meaty hand.

"Don't lie to me again. William Johnson. Where is he?"

She led him out to the other building, a kitchen with high, small windows, his hand on her shoulder and the pistol to her head. Inside the building was a big man with a round face and a broad nose. He looked up when the door opened and saw Arnita with Feeley's gun to her head.

"Are you William Johnson?"

"No sir."

"Bitch," Feeley pressed the muzzle of the gun to Arnita's temple.

"He take you to him! Tell him, Johnny, please!"

"Don't be hurting Arnita, sir. I take you to William."

Feeley stepped back and let her run out the door, and turned the gun on Johnny Davis.

"I got to drive you out there."

"Then do it. I'll be in the back seat with this gun, so don't get any ideas."

At the mill, Davis left the keys in the ignition of his car. He didn't produce the lantern, but led Feeley stumbling through the dark. They tripped up the stone steps and Davis unlocked the door. It scraped open when he pushed and then he slipped into the darkened interior and disappeared into the shadows among the ruined millworks. Feeley fired the gun, the bullet spanging off stone and thudding into old timber as he dodged away from the open door and the possibility of silhouetting himself. Furious, he considered taking Davis's car and driving away. Probably this was a snipe hunt. That possibility put him over the edge. He would kill Davis, and then find Arnita Lewis again and shoot her if he had to.

He crept deeper into the building. His eyes adjusted slowly, blue squares of dim moonlight appearing at the windows and streaming across the interior of the mill. He heard a creak in the dark and fired again. He changed position, staying in the shadows, taking cover behind the millstones. In the pale blue light he saw Davis break for a darkened, narrow staircase that descended to a lower level of the mill. Feeley took another shot, and missed, and charged after him.

Down in the lower level, the darkness was absolute. He took a few timid steps and decided he'd made a mistake. He heard a footstep on the stairs behind him and turned to fire, and something thudded into the back of his skull. His vision went white, and the pistol fell from his grip. He scrabbled after it on his hands and knees and took another blow to the back with what felt like a pipe or iron bar. He flailed wildly with his hands, caught a body, and flung it as hard as he could toward the stairs. The heap of arms and legs on the stairs floundered a moment, then found hands and knees and began to scramble back upstairs. Feeley dragged himself after it. He grabbed an ankle, took a foot to the face. Pulled harder, punched center mass. A wild kick caught him in the groin and he fell back, the man on the stairs scrambling upward.

Feeley collected himself and charged after him, upstairs, onto the millstone floor impaled on spears of moonlight. The hunched over form of Johnny Davis drew itself up to full height, the bar in his hand, raised above his head. Feeley dropped his shoulder and charged him, driving him back onto the millstones. The rage was black as death's cloak as it boiled up from his bowels. Feeley felt his face go slack as it burned with an electric cold, his lips quivering, his heart thudding in the barrel of his chest. He grabbed the wrist of Davis's weapon arm with one hand and his neck with the other and drove his skull down onto the millstone with every ounce of force he could summon. The sound was hollow and wet, the first blow probably fatal, but Feeley didn't stop until the rage was exhausted. In the back of his mind where his higher intelligence awaited the retirement of the savage in the driver's seat, he heard a car-motor start outside and saw the sweep of headlights pass the windows and disappear up the forest track. But that wasn't important just then. All that mattered was the fire in his chest and the stone in his gut, the throbbing in his loins, and the electric charge coursing through his skull. When it finally passed, he stood up, spit on what remained of Johnny Davis, and staggered out into the night.

It was a long walk back to the highway. He had to assume the man who drove off in the car was actually William Johnson. Davis had made a risky play, and it had half-worked. He had gotten Johnson out and stranded Feeley in the woods. Dying probably hadn't been part of his plan. Feeley could go find Arnita Lewis, but if she was smart, she was very far from her business. He'd need another way to draw Johnson out.

Monday I was back at work, stocking shelves for Mr. Clare, trying not to lose my mind at a case of three-piece steel cans of pineapple rings. Two-piece cans have the rounded bottom edge that fits into the rim of the top of another can, so they stack neatly and you could build a fortress out of them in the event of some strange grocery emergency. Three-piece cans, the top is the same as the bottom, with the same rim, and if you're extremely careful they stack right up until you get the last one ready, and then the whole thing collapses in an avalanche of canned goods and curse words, which had just happened for the second time.

"Well Mr. Cogbill."

I looked up to find Mrs. Carter standing over me with a shopping cart. She was wearing a heavy coat and a pair of flats, and although her hair and makeup were done she didn't look as put together as she had for her Garden Club meeting, which struck me as odd, but then so did the idea of a Garden Club meeting in November.

"Hello Mrs. Carter."

"What are you investigating today?" She said it coldly, sort of accusatory.

"I am also a grocery clerk."

"Does Mr. Clare know you go around peeping in keyholes when you aren't here?"

"I don't peep in keyholes."

"Well nevertheless you are certainly bothersome. I don't know what you said to Maynard the other day but he's a good provider and he means well."

"I never said he wasn't, Mrs. Carter."

"Well I hope you leave us alone now, Mr. Cogbill. I'll be speaking to Mr. Clare about you. I don't wish to cost you your job but this is deeply unsatisfactory."

She plowed through the middle of my pineapple cans and clipped my foot with the cart on her way by. I wondered how wealthy or educated or near to God one had to be to get the kind of job that didn't result in his fellow man treating him like something he'd chanced to tread upon in the seedy back alley of an Old West town where drunken adolescent cowboys pissed in gutters and whores in too much perfume strutted about on the back stairs with their tired bosoms spilling languidly out of vibrant corsets. But perhaps the reality of it was that it didn't matter your job. It may be that the majority of mankind bemoans his station and jumps at the first opportunity to step on his brother's face that he might taste for a moment the self-satisfaction of a Rockefeller or a DuPont.

For life itself was the product of an eons-long game of survival of the fittest, and from the first willful slime in the primordial soup to the Great Apes, all of evolution has led inexorably to the entitlement of man to throw his cigarette butts in urinals and his mate to drive her shopping buggy over the feet of men whose wits had already been bested by a case of tin cans. We are after all the same species who will butcher or enslave one another over a difference of creed, a disagreement of boundaries, or the very color of our flesh. To act as though man himself is not by nature red of tooth and claw is akin to playing the viola on the deck of a sinking ship.

But at the end of my shift I would punch my card and drive home to Ethel and make us supper, and we would pull the curtains and undress and lay together and the undeniable fact would be that happiness is where you make it, and you protect it with your life. That had been true since time began and would be until it ended, whether in this galaxy or the next.

When my shift ended it was mid-afternoon and I had a couple hours of daylight left. I kept thinking about Mrs. Carter. I did not much enjoy snooping into people's personal lives, but I also didn't enjoy being lied to, and it seemed to me that Laura Dawson had not been totally forthcoming about the nature of her relationship with Dane Harris. I used the phone booth around the side of the building facing the restaurant, a little box hunched in the cold under a utility pole against the whitewashed cinderblock wall.

"K Department."

"Miss Dawson?"

"Speaking."

"This is Harry Cogbill, I just have a couple of follow-up questions and then I'll be out of your hair."

"I've said all I care to say to you, Mr. Cogbill."

"I understand, but this isn't really about me, or you, is it? It's about Mildred Harris."

"Then perhaps you should bother her, Mr. Cogbill. I have a job to do."

"One last interview, please."

There was silence. I could feel her frustration coming down the line. I know I could have confronted her over the phone, but such things are rarely as effective in getting the truth out of someone, and I was ready to be done with this.

"The Post Office, Mr. Cogbill. Three o'clock."

I was going to have to hurry. North on 301 past Ralph Bunche to The Hillcrest Motel and its accompanying diner on the hilltop in Owens, down the long slope into the boggy crater, right onto Dahlgren Road, over the creek and into the burgeoning community outside the Naval base where a limping fugitive named Booth had once washed ashore on a farm belonging to Elizabeth Quesenberry, past the gas station and the elementary school, the little Methodist Church, and pulled up to the Post Office beside the guard box at the main gate to the Naval Weapons Lab.

I was a little late and I didn't see Miss Dawson's car. There was a young sailor smoking a cigarette and leaning on one of the pillars at the top of the Post Office steps trying to stay out of the wind, the enormous collars of his pea coat fluttering like dark sails, the anchors on his coat-buttons glowing like embers where they caught the sun. The shadows were already long and the sunlight dimming from gold to amber, but in the gloom of the portico I saw him straighten, push his dixie cup hat forward, and come down the steps like Popeye about to square up with Bluto the Terrible. I got out and leaned against the fender of the Pontiac and watched him toss his cigarette on the pavement as he approached.

"That's pretty good, but if you had a pipe you could sort of steam over here like a destroyer and really sell the image."

"Is your name Cogbill?"

"Sure, but you can call me Swee'Pea."

"Miss Dawson's not interested in whatever you're selling, mister."

"Cool it, Donald Duck. In the first place, I'm not selling anything. In the second, by the way you talk I'm guessing you're not her boyfriend, so what exactly is your angle?"

His face colored and he put a hand on my chest.

"Just back off, Cogbill."

"Seems to me you're the one offsides, kid. I'm just standing here. You approached me."

"I'm serious."

"Me too. Let's be clear. We're not on base. I was on the ground fighting Nazis in Europe when you were still playing with blocks. You have about thirty seconds to get your hands off me before you learn what Navy boot camp didn't teach you."

I almost felt bad. He was very young. His cheeks were flushed pink and his features were still sort of soft and boyish, but I saw his jaw working and resolve in his eyes as he lowered his hand.

"Just get out of here."

"Sure thing. Tell Miss Dawson something. Tell her I know."

"What's that supposed to mean?"

I'd gotten into my car and was pulling the door shut.

"Sorry kid. Maybe you should have started asking questions before you came on with the big dick act."

I left him standing there, hands in his coat pockets, a navy blue silhouette against the mandarin sky.

Ethel had picked up the mail from John and among the usual assortment of bills and correspondences from her relatives, there was a plain envelope with my name and no return address.

Inside was a piece of paper that said simply: "Salem Tuesday 5pm" and was signed "MW."

That night I glazed pork chops in orange marmalade and the yield from a pomegranate I worked over with an orange juicer, and cooked the chops with cloves and a sprig of rosemary. We had leftover green beans and mashed potatoes on the side. Fawkes as always voiced his displeasure at being excluded from this feast.

"This Dane Harris thing is doing a fine job of reminding me that I'm not a private investigator."

"You cain't let it bother you if you make some folks mad."

"Sure, but it might bother Mr. Clare if his customers are complaining about his employees."

"Seems like Dane was probably having an affair. That's what Millie hired you to find out. You could call it here."

"I think Millie hired me to find out that it wasn't happening."

"But it was."

"Maybe."

"Seems like it."

"Yeah."

"You're not convinced."

"It just doesn't make sense. Laura Dawson was able to convince a fresh-faced young sailor to come threaten me this afternoon."

"Women can get guys to do all sorts of things. We learn it when we're little. We just get better at it."

"That's exactly my point. She has a world full of single young men to choose from. She's gonna pick Dane? I'm not buying it."

"Dane was a nice man."

I didn't say anything.

"You're right, Cogbill."

"Something's off about Maynard and his wife, too."

"Mrs. Carter does sound awfully defensive."

"Does the Garden Club meet in November?"

"I don't know, I'm not in the damn Garden Club."

"She was all dressed up."

"Women dress up for each other, Hieronymus. Nobody wants to be the ugly duckling."

"I know."

"My mama used to curl her hair to go to the Post Office, in case she ran into any of her friends."

"Mrs. Carter didn't put quite as much effort into dressing for the supermarket."

"Well the Garden Club's a little more exclusive."

"If they even meet in November."

We both jumped as someone started pounding on the door. Fawkes came barreling in from his pen, raced through the house in a silver blur, and through the bedroom door. I knew without looking that he'd gone under the bed.

"Stay here, Ethel."

I grabbed the shotgun and went to the door. Maynard Carter was on the porch, a steak knife in his hand.

"Miss Dawson called me. She said you figured it out."

I began to suspect I hadn't figured out much of anything.

"Carter. You want to put the knife down."

"What, you haven't finished ruining me yet?"

"I haven't done anything to you, Maynard."

"Maybe not yet. What happens when you tell Mildred about Dane and me?"

I felt stupid. Slow.

"I didn't mean for Dane to die. His heart just stopped. It was, it was his first time. Y'know. With a man."

"What's the knife for?"

He held it, trembling, to his wrist.

"Lillian and the kids'll have the money."

I lowered the shotgun. "I haven't told them, Maynard. I don't care if you're gay. It's not my business. You don't want to do this."

"It isn't logical, that I'm the way I am. I'm a mathematician, I-I'm accustomed to things making sense."

"Okay, so some things aren't logical. I can't solve your problems for you, but I won't make them worse. Okay? I'll tell Millie there was nothing to learn. Dane was alone."

I felt awful. This was why it was better not to pry into people's business. Why I didn't want to take Mildred's case to begin with. I doubted any good ever came of fidelity cases.

"Why should I believe you?"

"Because I believe you. There was no foul play in Dane's death. Whatever happened between you and him is beyond mattering at this point. Telling Millie wouldn't make her feel any better. All it would do is hurt her, and you, and I have no reason to do that. You're a logical guy, so you see that, right?"

"What about the money Millie's paying you?"

"I have a day job, Maynard. You don't believe me you can ask your wife, she ran over my foot with her shopping cart. I didn't want Mildred's money in the first place."

"You're serious?"

"He's serious." It was Ethel. She'd come to the door.

"You know Harry, Dane liked you. Both of you. He admired your relationship. He said he'd never had that, not with Millie."

"I think he tried to tell me that. At the Fall Festival."

"He trusted you," Maynard said. "Don't let us down."

CHAPTER FIFTEEN

THE NEXT EVENING as the sun sank into the West I chased my harpoon of a shadow out Route 3 to Shiloh and turned by Parker's Store in Index, into the deepening gloom among the twisted winter trees, over Jett's Creek and into the small clearing where the little brick church with its crowned belfry sat atop its hill. I had been to the bank and got my Colt 1911 out of the lockbox in safe deposit, and its weight in the hip pocket of my mackinaw made it feel lopsided and awkward on my shoulders.

By now it was full dark, and the cloud cover blotted out the sky except for the dull glow of the moon and a hazy golden light that encircled it like the rings of Saturn. I pulled up to the church thinking I was too soon because the building was dark and there were no cars in the lot. A tap on the window of the passenger door made me jump. Then I saw Marion Washington's face as he leaned down to peer through the glass. I leaned across the passenger area and pulled up on the little chrome golf tee that operated the door lock. Marion climbed in and pulled the door shut.

"Pull around back, man. Cut the lights."

"Marion what the hell's going on?"

"I get out this car right now. Or you do what I tell you. Don't make no nevermind to me."

He was unarmed and his voice was calm, his lips slightly pursed under his pencil-thin moustache, his eyebrows raised. He was neatly dressed and smelled of fresh cologne. I did what he said. Around back of the church was the green Dodge pickup, the lights off and the dull yellow of the moon gleaming off the wax.

From under a tarp or blanket in the back, a dark sinewy figure with bushy hair. He slid in the backseat of my Pontiac and in the mirror I could see behind the scrubby beard the familiar face of William Johnson.

"Mr. Harry."

"William. Please don't call me Mister. It makes me uncomfortable."

"I'm sorry Mr. Harry."

"I'm glad to see you're alive. Why are you still in the county?"

"I got to see to bidness. Yes sir I do."

"What business is that, William?"

"Best you don't know."

"Look, William, if you killed George Siever I know you were acting under duress. You might could tell the sheriff and—"

"Man, come on. What I'm 'posed to tell him? I done kilt a white man. He ain't gone care why."

"You're better than that, William."

"What if I ain't?"

"You're better than that. It's Boone."

"What you know about Boone?"

"I know he's a bad man. I know he used to run drugs and girls out at the Beach."

"He's the devil, Mr. Harry."

"What did he do to you? Did he threaten you?"

"He don't threaten like that, out in the open. He don't talk straight to nobody. He come at you crooked like, you only see the threat out the corner your eye."

I thought I understood what he meant.

"My daddy used to help farm the land out Nanzatico, maintain the estate, before Mr. Boone bought it. But Boone don't care 'bout farming. Sold off most the farmland. He ain't got nothing for to pay Daddy or me. He charge us rent."

"You didn't have anywhere else to go?"

"Nowhere we wouldn't have to pay for, no sir. And our family done always lived at Nanzatico. Daddy too proud to leave. Boone give Esther a job. Clean the house. My sister." I heard the tension in his voice. I never even knew he had a sister.

"Where is she, William?"

"She were happy at first, clean the big house, get paid reg'lar. Pretty soon he offer a job out the Beach. But she seem sad. Wouldn't never say why. It was like he done pulled the light right out her eyes. One day she ain't come home. Boone said...said she moved to Balt'more. We ain't heard from her since."

My stomach felt hollow and cold.

"He promise me I do this favor for him, Mr. Harry, and he bring Esther home. I knowed he were lyin'. But that's my baby sister. That's my baby sister."

"William you've got to tell this to Jay Powell."

"He ain't gone care about a colored girl get turned out by a rich white man. No sir. And he ain't gone care why I done what I done. Cain't a nigga catch a break. Not in this world."

"William, were you with Joey DeLarosa in the woods behind my house?"

"I'm sorry Mr. Harry. He thought you would help us."

"I'd have helped you, William. If I can, I still will."

"Cain't nobody help me."

"You came to talk to me. That's more than I expected."

"Mr. Joey dead."

"I know."

"Him that got him, he work for Boone?"

"For a man named Adagio. And maybe Boone too."

"He still lookin' for me."

"You should leave the county, William."

"No sir. They threatening my daddy I don't come to them."

"I'll see to Mr. Micah." It was the first time Marion had spoken.

"You cain't go there, M. It ain't safe."

"I'll go." A strange calm had come over me.

Marion's head came a quarter-turn toward me. "Why?"

I wasn't sure how to answer. It wasn't a white or black thing, and it wasn't a from-here or come-here thing. Hell, I was a come-here. Maybe deep in some fortified, private spiritual place, I still believed that men could be good or evil and that any of us had the ability to judge such things clearly as though we were not ourselves guilty of personal atrocities the shame of which haunted us in the quiet moments when we lay awake with nothing but our conscience and the voice of the Holy Spirit whispering in our ear. Now that's a lie. I walked daily with shame and guilt and I had carried it with me since a whiteout day in Ardennes shrouded in a chill like the breath of the damned who slouched in darkened windows of ancient homes and hung around the gnarled roots of weathered trees, waiting to rise from the mists and walk again upon the world they had betrayed.

Or maybe Frank Burkitt had my measure after all. Maybe I was a fraud and a son of a bitch and when the moment came I'd freeze and let another man die in my place, another son bleed out in the rubble of man's inhumanity to man. Maybe the war was never over. Maybe there was only ever one war, and it had begun with Cain and Abel, and would end with time itself.

I inclined my head and caught Marion's eye.

"Because I want to."

I double-checked my pistol was loaded and cocked, round chambered, safety on, and dropped it back in the pocket of my mackinaw. William had insisted on riding with me. He was willing to trade his life for his daddy's, but I suspected Micah might prefer it the other way around. I screwed my fedora down low against the cold, and turned up my collar, but the icy wind made my eyes water and my nose run. We left my car by the side of a narrow road so old it remembered the rattle of wagon wheels, the stamp of hooves, and the odor of hot horse manure. We crossed a bog and entered a forest.

I was back in France, the Chateau on its hilltop under the Nazi flag, the stormtroopers patrolling the grounds in their buckets and red armbands, Mausers and MP 40s over their shoulders or clenched in pale hands as my unit entered the village below. The fellows from my platoon were spread around me through the trees, mud on their gaiters, M1s held to their chests, faces invisible in the shadow of their steel pots. Above the outstretched claws of naked trees, the moon hid her pale form demurely behind a lacy cloud. A light rain began to fall. Rollie was beside me, his eyes wide as they moved carefully around the grounds, looking for danger. But that's wrong, Rollie and I hadn't met yet. I looked again, and there he was. Hadn't I left Europe years ago?

That wasn't the chateau ahead of me, it was Nanzatico. The soldiers around me melted into the mist like sand sculptures in the surf. William Johnson was thirty or forty yards away to my right, picking his way through the trees. I was in Virginia. In King George. Rollie's home. Then the implacable silence was laid open with a shot, and shards of wood stripped out of the black walnut tree beside me. I dropped into the mud and rolled into an icy stream, peering between crooked holly saplings and whips of greenbrier into the faintly glowing mist, looking for the gunman, but I could see no sign of him.

I crept through the corn stubble. I had lost sight of William, but it was his home and he knew the land better than I ever would. We were west of the big house, a dark line of trees between us and the bay, so I picked my way toward the cover they provided and began working my way toward the Johnson house. I heard no further shots and indeed no sound at all, save for the water lapping at the logs along the edge of the bay and the occasional faint splash of river life.

There was a strange, pale flickering from the windows of Micah's cabin. When I got close enough to look through the window, there was footage of a young black woman cast on the wall from an 8mm projector. She was undressed, cleaning a mantel with a feather duster as a white man whose face was never shown groped her and slapped her bottom. I could tell from her features that she must be Esther Johnson. I could see no one in the house. I hoped Micah hadn't seen the film.

I crept up onto the small porch and found the door unlocked. I kept my pistol at the ready and moved methodically through the cabin. It was little more than a shotgun house, having been wired for electricity and partitioned into a few small rooms with meager furnishings. More than once I thought I saw the dark shape of a man in the shadows but each time I would look again and there was nothing there. I stepped back outside and into the trees.

Nanzatico stood brooding over the yards, among the magnolias and willows, its namesake, Nanzatico Bay, glowing softly
behind it in the diffuse moonlight. A single lighted window like
a yellow eye peered at me from the mansion, the white castle of
a long-dead feudal lord surrounded by the humble dwellings of
his serfs and peasants, the shallow beauties of his legacy written
in the graceful symmetry of the home, and the stench of its rotten heart still echoing in the treatment of black men and women,
in the abuses of power that kept the poor in the dirt while the
rich built more palaces on more hilltops and along more shore-
lines, funded by the stolen income of the working class.

The seat of power had just shifted from a morally and literally bankrupt southern aristocracy, to a northern fraternity of
modern-day pirates and highwaymen, warlords who laundered
dirty money by investing in shoddy housing for middle-class
southerners they viewed as backwards and ignorant. The oldest
lie in the world is that another man will ever feel responsible for
your welfare, that he will provide adequately for it, or that those
in power will make him do so. Every poor southerner, white or
black, learned long ago that nothing in the world belongs to us
unless we make or buy it for ourselves; that the promises of lead-
ers will always disappear in ash and smoke and in their world we
will never be more than chattel, regardless under whose flag we
march. Unless you are your own master, you are not free.

There were several outbuildings — a smokehouse, summer
kitchen, the plantation office — all sort of clustered around the
circular drive in front of the big house. The red-roofed barn
across the yard from Micah's house. Crouched beneath the
boughs at the edge of the treeline along the bay was an old
springhouse, set well back from the rest.

The creaking door sounded like Armageddon as I hauled it open. I stood aside and waited, knowing if anyone was inside with a weapon, they'd see me in the open doorway long before I'd see them, even in the dark of night. There was a whimper from inside. I checked my six and then got down on my belly and peered through the doorway. Micah's one arm was tied to one of the beams. He was dirty and disheveled, and I could see he had been beaten. He was alone.

I slipped down into the springhouse and untied his wrist.

"Mr. Cogbill? They lukin' for William."

"They're using you as bait. You've got to get out of here."

"Where William at?"

"I'll get you to my car, we can go to the Sheriff and tell him everything these guys did to you."

"Where William at?"

"Looking for you. Can you walk?"

"If them men get aholt of him they'll kill him."

"I know. I'm going to go after him, but I need you to get to the car." I told him where we'd left it.

"Stick to the trees. It's dark and they won't be able to see you. Stay low if you can. Don't go to your house. Don't look inside. Okay?"

I cautiously looked out the door and gave him the all-clear. Then I helped him up through the door and cursed as he took off toward the summer kitchen a short distance away. He peeled off around the side furthest from the big house, past the tool shed toward the red-roofed barn, not at all in the direction I'd wanted him to go. As I went after him I felt the mission slipping away, my sense of insufficiency for this or any moment sweeping back over me like a black tide.

I saw a hulking shadow separate from a tree and melt into the low shape of the barn a hundred yards ahead. Then the moon slipped behind a cloud like a black satin pillow, the light seeping around it like molten butter in an iron skillet. Down among the trees the shadows deepened and the night swallowed the forest and the gunman and me, until only the baleful window-eye of Nanzatico remained.

I knew Micah was heading into trouble, so I rose from cover and fired a few rounds at the place I'd seen the large silhouette that was likely Eamon Feeley. He returned fire and I threw myself back into the mud and hoped his attention was diverted enough to miss Micah sprinting across the darkened field to his left. From the sound of it, Feeley had a rifle, which meant his chances of hitting anything at range were a lot better than mine. I crept among the buildings in the yard, staying low as possible, trying to keep my teeth from chattering. The misty rain kept getting in my eyes and my clothes were muddy and damp and I blinked, trying to clear my vision.

The mist clung to the ground like a layer of frost, like dry ice, heavy and thick, and I thought I saw men around me in battle-dress, gaiters and steel pots, belly-crawling beside me as we advanced on the gunman's position. I could hear the panzers in the distance, the artillery jolting the earth and shattering the faces of buildings old enough to remember feudal lords. Lieutenant Carlisle was yelling for us to follow him, and somewhere behind, sarge was barking at us to crawl faster, were we maggots or were we men. Brinny and Jacks were setting up Ma Deuce in a shallow depression they'd dug out in the mud, Brinny on his back, ready to feed belts of bulky .50 cal rounds to Jacks on the gun. I could hear someone shouting in German ahead in the darkness. They had William, and we had to get him back.

I reached up to clamp the pot down on my head, and touched felt. Where was my rifle? I'd lost my helmet and my rifle. As good as dead. No, the war was over. Long over. But the supine figures in the mist were still there. I exhaled, and something landed on my hat brim and slipped into my hand: a toothpick. I looked up as the moon slid out from behind the cloud. Through the mist I could see Feeley standing over me holding a rifle. William was next to me, looking him in the eye. I honestly don't know why Feeley didn't shoot; he looked as surprised as I was. I had a split-second to react. I shot without really aiming and got Feeley through the inner portion of his left thigh, near the groin.

There is a strange pause before a body starts to bleed in earnest. Feeley slid down on his ass and slithered into the mud, and then the blood came out of him in a steady pulse and I knew I'd severed his femoral artery. The color drained out of his face and inexplicably he didn't scream or yell.

I struggled to wipe the rain from my eyes and realized the black man standing above me wasn't William at all, but Rollie Taylor, evaporating into an electric blue haze. Feeley's voice gasped out faintly, and though I've never been sure I'd swear his final words were, "they're all dead." I have never cared to reflect on what that meant.

I finally managed to wipe my eyes on the inside of my jacket, and seeing no one in the moonlit field around me, I took off for the barn. I pressed myself against the side and listened. Long moments passed with no more shooting and finally I heard Boone's voice.

"Eamon! Eamon, tell me you got him."

A few more moments passed, my heart pounding in my throat.

Then Tom Boone appeared, with Micah Johnson in front of him. He had Johnson's one hand wrenched around behind him so the old man's body was twisted at an angle out in front of him, creating enough space to get the shotgun pressed into Micah's chin.

"That you, Willy? I told you what would happen. Thought you loved your daddy. It's a pity. Just can't trust a colored boy to act civilized."

I stepped out of the shadows, my pistol raised.

"Drop the shotgun, Boone. It's over."

"Cogbill. You killed Feeley?"

"If you harm that old man, you're next."

"See, that's where you're wrong. Jimmie Vasiliou told me all about you. How you couldn't shoot a Nazi. How you let a poor colored boy jump on a grenade and got all broke up about it. You're nothing, Cogbill."

"I'm not the one hiding behind a human shield, Boone."

"Mr. Cogbill you got to help William find my daughter. Just shoot this man. Shoot him t'rew me if you got to, I'm old, I'on't care no more. Help my children, sir. Please!"

"You're wasting your breath, Micah," Boone said. "It won't happen."

I knew if I lowered my weapon or turned my back, he'd use the shotgun on me. Boone wasn't stupid. Micah Johnson was no threat to him. And we both knew I would never risk harming Micah. What I didn't know was where William was, but I didn't think Boone knew either, and that was the only advantage we had. He couldn't risk turning his back on me. As it turned out, William was thinking along the same lines.

A dark form coagulated out of the mist behind Boone. There was a sound like a shovel breaking through clay and striking stone; then Boone sagged, and gasped a rattling sigh. Micah Johnson stumbled forward and Boone pulled the trigger as he fell. The blast went wild, echoing in the wet air. William stood there, holding a sickle he must have taken from the barn and wearing most of Boone's blood.

"William..."

"Tell Sheriff I done it."

"I'll tell him you saved your father."

"We bot' know it won't matter none. You think I get a fair trial cos some ol' yella piece a paper say I'm 'posed to?"

"I'll tell him..."

"And he look at me see a nigga wit' blood on his clothes and start tying the damn rope."

"Run, William."

We looked at each other a moment, and then he turned and disappeared into the night. He was right. It had to end. The State would kill him for what he'd done, and it would just be more of the same. There'd been enough. What was the State, after all, but another gang of hoods forcing people to do their bidding under threat of violence? What was law and order but the fascist's form of coercion?

We could pass more laws and try to pretend anyone who looked like William was free, but they wouldn't be, nor anyone else, until we learned to stop giving power to a ruling class. Maybe we never would. Maybe in the end we're just a herd of panicked horses seeking shelter from a fire inside the very barn it consumes.

The last I saw of William Johnson, he and his father were in Boone's boat, a soft white shape fading into the mist on Nanzatico Bay. I don't know where they ended up, but I like to imagine William found his sister, and that perhaps like my ancestor

Charles Christian Cogbill, he made it to a place where he could start anew and live in dignity, and find love and raise his children as men and women who were truly free.

The next day, when Powell had secured a warrant, he and some state police officers raided the Ernest Pie. Adagio and the Vittorio brothers had fled. The file cabinets had been emptied. So had the safe. When they arrived at Nanzatico they found Agents Cathy and Douglas and a few federal crime scene guys crawling around.

"Good morning, sheriff."

"You boys find anything?"

"Nothing you need to concern yourself with." Agent Cathy had a styrofoam coffee cup in his hand and a cigarette clamped between two fingers of the same hand, held a little away from the cup. His gunmetal hair fluttered faintly in the morning breeze, and his trouser cuffs rippled at his ankles.

"It's my county, fellas."

"But not your case. Whyn't you take the day, go hunting or whatever you boys do out here."

Powell got in Cathy's grey face. They were about the same height, Powell a shade burlier. His nostrils flared and his eyes narrowed. "Now you ain't gonna come in my county and talk down to me, I don't give a damn whose badge you're carrying."

"Careful, sheriff. You lay one finger on me and I'll have your badge and chuck you in a hole you won't get out of. I know your reputation."

Behind him, they were loading a wrapped body into a van.

"Who is that? What happened here?"

"One of your citizens. Mr. Boone."

"Listen boys, someone took out the trash last night. Hector Adagio was doing business out of a restaurant on 301. He's disappeared. He and Boone were associated."

"We know."

"Look, I'm trying to find a man named Feeley in connection with the murder of a Caroline man named—"

"Joey DeLarosa. Like I said, it's not your case. Joey was a Federal asset, you were already warned to stay away. Any information you have on this case, you'll have to turn it over to us."

"Oh, gotdammit."

I kept my word to Maynard Carter. I tried to give Mildred Harris her money back on the grounds that I'd found nothing, but she wouldn't take it and I finally had to drive home feeling like I'd ripped her off, something I expressed to Ethel that afternoon as we took our coffee in front of the fire.

"I don't think you ripped her off, Cogbill. She wanted peace of mind, and I reckon you gave it to her."

"On a lie."

"Well it ain't a perfect world."

"Parts of it are."

"I do like this part very damned much," Ethel said.

"Me too."

One day Ethel woke up sick and could keep nothing down. I came home from work with chicken and broth, veggies and egg noodles, but even my homemade soup did not cure her. All day her stomach revolted and into the night and the next day and so on for a week. About all she could keep down was water.

Toward the end of the week Frank stopped by. He turned his hat by the brim in his hands and did not say much to me when I opened the door, but I invited him in and hung around the kitchen while he visited with Ethel. When he came back down the hall I walked him to the front door.

"I'm sorry for the way I treated you, Cogbill. You don't have to forgive me. But I think for both our sakes, and for Ethel's, we need to forgive ourselves for our own pasts."

For a moment I wondered what planet I was on.

"You're probably right, Frank. What brought this on?"

"I don't want to get into it. I just realized while I was in the hospital that I don't want to spend the little time I have left on this earth cutting myself off from the only family I have. That means Ethel, and it means you too. If you're still willing to give me a chance."

"Frank I'm glad to."

"When Alice died, I was maybe too busy being a big strong stupid man. I let Ethel down. Don't you let her down. Don't be a big strong stupid man. Be whatever she needs you to be."

"Yes sir."

He stuck his hand out, and I took it, and we shook and then he turned and walked out and closed the door behind him, and I stood there a moment looking at the door as the muscles in my neck and shoulders relaxed like the unfurling of rose petals. It was a long moment and the sun seemed to emerge from the clouds like dawn on the first Easter, and I felt inexplicably the divine hand lift me up as I had once lifted an abandoned fox kit in a field, and I understood the power of submission and of humility, and grace.

"I forgive you, Frank."

CHAPTER SIXTEEN

I WAS OUTSIDE in my mackinaw and battered brown fedora, my breath huffing out in dense white clouds as the ax head dropped and split another log. The sky was a slab of steel, the air heavy, crisp and clear, the fields devoid of color but for the last speckled leaves of the yellow poplar that skated across the grass when the wind blew. Nearby Fawkes prowled his pen with the kind of smile that made me worry what mischief was in his heart.

Ethel's red F-1 groaned on its springs as it clattered over the cattleguard and traced the dry orange ruts of the drive like a locomotive on its tracks. She circled around in front of the house and took her accustomed spot beside my Pontiac. My wife stepped down off the running board, clamping her hat to her head with one gloved hand, her woolen coat, bell-like, hiding the cut of her waist as it spread across the swell of her hips. I stuck the ax in the next log and admired her legs in her nylons, and the way her smile lit the yard like spring. With the other hand she chunked shut the door of the truck and crossed the yard to me, all chestnut curls and electric blue eyes, the spray of freckles across her nose somewhat faded with the arrival of winter.

"What did the doctor say?"

"Well, the bad news is we're gonna have to really manage our money from now on."

I felt a chill unconnected to the weather. A slideshow of horrors passed before my eyes too quickly to register. I thought

I might black out. I took her in my arms, and held her, and in the back of my head demanded the Lord not take her from me, anything but her. Anything up to and including my own life. I took a deep breath.

"How bad is it?"

Her voice came back muffled from the front of my coat.

"Oh it ain't so bad, Cogbill. A few months of discomfort and everything'll be good. We'll just have to accept that our lives'll be different from now on."

I couldn't breathe. It was all I could do not to cry.

"The diagnosis, Ethel."

"Hieronymus, I'm tryin' to say I'm pregnant."

It hit me like a marching band where every instrument was playing a different tune. Although relieved, for some reason I thought with sadness of our summer picnics at the edge of the forest, the pale, thick curves of Ethel's nakedness soft and warm in my arms beneath the blue dome of Heaven. Soon our privacy would become a commodity, and our physical love a thing of the past.

"Well Cogbill, say somethin'. Seein' as I just come from the doctor, reckon I had about enough of waiting for today."

"It's a lot to process."

"Think how I feel."

I kissed her, took the hat from her head and buried my face in the strawberry scent of her hair.

"You're right, I'm sorry Ethel. Of course I'm happy. I think."

She pushed away from me, looked up at me with a glare that could have melted the face off a dragon.

"Got to say, this ain't goin' like I expected."

with hands almost too cold to function; the click of the zippo sounded like a hammer on a nail in the cold air.

"Jesus Christ, Rollie, I can't feel my nuts."

He took a long drag, perhaps in a vain attempt to warm himself. The cherry of the cigarette swelled brighter, reflecting in his eyes and casting a red glow across his chocolate-colored skin as he knocked the snow off his boots with the stock of his rifle.

"Don't wanna lose that shit Rony, they property of the US government. Take 'em out your pension."

Rony was short for Hieronymus I guess. Rollie and Rony, Europe's garbage men. The pay was lousy, but at least the commute was terrible.

"It get this cold in King George, Rollie?"

"Nah man. Not really. Some nights in February it be a lil rough, I guess. But not like this. Build you a fire, if it too cold you can sleep by the hearth, curled up on the flo'. Lot of hills up where I live at. Good sledding for the little ones. But it don't snow every winter. Ain't no different in Chesterfield, is it?"

"Probably not."

"Why ain't you like Chesterfield, Rony?"

"Baggage. Family stuff, man."

"You go see 'em if you get out this joint?"

"I don't know. I don't guess we get along all that well."

"Brother, is all white guys this damn sad?"

"I don't know. Probably not."

By the next morning the growl of the panzers had reached us, the air was full of smoke and ash, and pieces of exploding trees, the sound of gunfire and detonating ordnance a physical force with weight and mass all its own. My teeth rattled, the ringing in my ears the only sound not muffled by my ruptured eardrums.

"I'm delighted we're having a child. I'm terrified what w
bringing her into."

"I don't reckon the world's ever been unicorns and rainb
Cogbill."

I knew she was right. The shadows were long and blue
der the distant droplet of molten gold that was the winter
I walked with her into the house, and made grilled cheese
tomato soup and a pot of coffee, and we ate in relative si
as Fawkes stood under the table, looking expectantly from
to the other of us, his long snout and twinkling eyes quiv
with grilled cheese envy.

After dinner I walked out across the darkened fields u
moon that seemed somehow brighter than the sun, wreatl
a fat corona in the chilly, humid air. The arthritic fingers
winter trees clawed at the velvet sky, the wind pulling my
and the brim of my hat as the snow began to fall. The wh
hit like the fist of God, painting the frozen earth with th
of urgency and intent only attributable to divine consciou
I had been here before, in December '44. I could smel
ite in the air, hear the crescendo screams of mortar she
the distant snarl of tank engines. I pulled the army-issu
tighter around my neck, tugged on the belt at my waist t
it closer to my body. The wool cap I wore under the st
was slipping upward again, off my ears, and I tugged it
The fingers were cut off my gloves so I could shoot,
couldn't feel my fingertips. We were running our M1's
lube to keep them from freezing up.

I was dug in a foxhole with Rollie Taylor, our eyes w
and our noses running. He fumbled a cigarette out of

I remember little with clarity: the tanks making the earth tremble, the screams of dying men on both sides, the odor of feces and the metallic tang of blood mingling with the cordite and the pine. A distant rattle, and the muted sound of Rollie's voice, yelling something. In the muddy snow between us landed a German grenade, a long wooden handle with a small, olive-colored canister riveted to the top. I hesitated half a second. I saw Rollie fall on it as somebody tackled me with a hit that would have done an NFL linebacker proud, my steel pot wheeling away into the trees as a muted thump ended my best friend's life.

I clawed my way out of the snow, my head still ringing, and looked down and saw the red plaid of my mackinaw. I had made it out of Europe once again. I shivered, and a steady, low-voltage current coursed through me, from the crown of my head to the tips of my toes. A wisp of electric blue smoke curled among the trees, seemingly undisturbed by the whistling wind and the whirling snow. Where the blue smoke crossed the strands of moonlight, I could see part of him, the cigarette clamped between the fingers of his dangling hand, the collar of his olive-colored jacket turned against the wind.

"War's over, Rony."

"Gonna be a father."

"So take your ass home."

"What if I'm no good at it?"

"What if you is?"

"Sometimes when I fail, people die."

"You didn't let me die. I saved you. If I'd knowed you be all tore up about it, I'd've let you punch your ticket instead."

"I know you better than that."

"Don't get me wrong, man, I wanted to live. Sometime it just don't work out the way we want."

"That's what I'm afraid of."

"Naw. What you afraid is sometime it do."

The blue smoke dissipated, and my friend was gone.

I had no idea from which way I'd come. I'd been in the same spot in the woods for an indefinite amount of time; the snow was driving, and any tracks I might have made in the beginning were covered and blown away.

My ears were numb, and my face felt raw, my nose and eyes watering as they had in The Ardennes so many years ago. I gathered the collar of my mackinaw close around my neck and jaw, and through the thin fabric of my trousers, my manhood had retracted and now hid, like an animal burrowed in its lair. In the whiteout conditions I couldn't see far, no lights or familiar land features to guide my way. I listened for any sound but could hear nothing over the wind and the tinkling of snow.

I began to walk; any movement to generate body heat was better than sitting still, and any direction better than none. The snow had gathered in my eyelashes and I had to squint to keep it out of my eyes. Dark, furtive movement ahead in the underbrush, and a grey fox appeared.

"Fawkes?"

The fox looked at me, his back frosted with snow, and trotted at a leisurely pace off to the right. I followed him, not knowing what else to do.

"Is that you, buddy? How'd you get out here?"

The wind pushed the dry snow like foaming surf in wavelets across the ground, and the tracks were fading before my eyes. I hurried on after my vulpine guide, and twice saw him waiting for me at the edge of my vision. At last the forest ended and he led me across an ocean of snow, until I saw familiar fences and the dim yellow eye of our living-room window where the house crouched on a slight rise in the open fields. I wiped my eyes on the inside of my collar, and when I cleared them the fox was gone, and so were his tracks, and I had no explanation but for the wind and the snow.

I stumbled onward to my house, with its chimney-smoke scattering in the curling winds, past the igloo-like mounds of the cars, and climbed onto the porch, where briefly a silhouette appeared at a window. The door opened and my wife pulled me into the warm yellow light. Fawkes was curled up asleep on the couch.

"My God, Hieronymus!"

She helped me undress and stood with me under a hot shower and held me until the blue tinge faded from my skin, and my anatomy more or less restored itself to its usual configuration.

"Were you trying to die, or just flirting with it?"

"I had to figure some things out."

"You ain't sure you want to have a baby with me."

"Christ, Ethel, of course I do."

"Then what the hell's the problem?"

"Me. The world."

"I'm part of that world."

"But so was Nestor Lazos, so was Hitler. So are Hector Adagio and the men who pushed William to kill an innocent man. The same world that gave you to me, took Rollie Taylor's life in a place that still haunts my nightmares."

I turned the water off, and we dried ourselves. She brought me a big, heavy blanket and wrapped me in it, then put on her bathrobe and led me back to the living room and the warmth of our hearth.

"A baby, Ethel. How am I supposed to protect her from all of this?"

"In the first place, you don't have to do it alone, and you know it. Why did you ask me to marry you?"

"The morning you drove up here was like the first time I saw the sun."

She poked at the embers and added another log, and the blue-and-red coals reached out in yellow tongues to consume it.

"You're going to be an incredible mother. We'll just have to make do with whatever kind of daddy I turn out to be."

"You think you'll screw it up?"

"I do most things."

"Show me somebody who doesn't. Hieronymus, my daddy hadn't got much ability to discuss his feelings. I think he's afraid of being vulnerable. It took me a couple decades to figure that out. I thought it was me. For a long time. I ran around got in trouble just trying to get noticed."

I held her tight, and kissed her hair.

"And then I met you."

"And I am also a big strong stupid pain in the ass."

"Maybe sometimes. But you know how to love."

"I get it wrong too."

"But that don't stop you from doing it anyway. And no matter how mean the world is, we own this little corner of it, you and me and Fawkes, and baby too. We're a team. We don't give up on each other."

"I couldn't. Any more than I could quit breathing."

"That's how I know you're gonna be a great daddy. So don't get all twisted up. Don't overthink."

"Rollie thinks I'm scared of things going well."

She eyed me curiously. "Rollie died in Europe, remember?"

The next day, after a hot breakfast we cleaned off the truck and warmed up the motor while we had a second pot of coffee. Then we bundled up and drove to Hud Avery's place on Owens Drive, up on the ridgeline behind the old airport that was being turned into a residential subdivision. Below us, construction equipment and a couple of half-finished houses stood covered in snow in a semicircle near a flat expanse of white that had once been a grass runway. All Ethel would tell me was that she wanted to share something special with me.

Avery's house sat along the lip of an ancient, boggy crater that encompassed the Dahlgren area on the southern bank of the Potomac River. The intersection of US Route 301 and State Highway 206 was in the bottom beyond a scrubby treeline. The Morgantown Bridge was visible to the north. A hundred yards from Avery's house, a gnarled old tree stood at the precipice of the hill, and his fields lay spread like a blanket below. The peak of his roof stuck out black against the snow that had drifted in his gutters, and the broad gable across the back of the house was split by a tall, red-brick chimney. It gave forth a steady, peaceful stream of grey smoke in the clear mid-morning light, the yellow sun shining off the fallen snow with all the hope and glory of the grace of God.

When Avery opened his door, his chocolate lab shot out into the driveway like a ballistic missile, kicking up snow with his big powerful feet and flopping over on his back to roll around in it.

"God damn it, Buck, get in here!"

The dog nearly tackled us all as he came charging back, shaking himself off at the door. Hud shook my hand and hugged Ethel, offered us both coffee, and approved Ethel's request to borrow his taboggan for old-time's sake.

"Little old for sledding, ain't you?"

I nodded and chose not to elaborate. That he still so
times visited me was not something I ever chose to share, e
with the one person in this world who knows my soul. B
wondered if he didn't have a point: my grip on happiness
tenuous. Every change in the wind, every chance or happ
stance could take it all back without warning or mercy; I I
never quite accepted that the world could be a place of warn
and hope, except for those brief moments in Ethel's embra
when our bodies were as joined as our hearts and souls and I f
fleetingly, that I was part of a larger universe, in the sight of
just and loving God.

"Well hell, Cogbill, I've always told you that."

"What's that?"

"That yer afraid to be happy."

"I'm afraid of losing my happiness."

"So you push it away preemptively."

"I guess."

"Well stop it, because the baby and I are going to want y
around."

"Me too. Only I guess our picnics are going to be a li
different."

"Hieronymus Cogbill, that is why the good Lord m
babysitters."

My wife has always been smarter than I am.

"You still cold?"

"A little."

She stretched out beside me and opened her robe.

"Well, I cain't get any more pregnant."

I could find no fault with her logic.

"Well, I'm inclined to think so..."

"Oh now, Mr. Avery. Cogbill here needs to live a little, and we've reason to celebrate."

I stuck my hands in my pockets and grinned as she broke the news.

"We're havin' a baby."

"Well, hell, congratulations. You be careful on that sled then, won't you?"

She promised, and I promised to make sure of it, and then we dragged the sled out to the brink of the hilltop, and I had to admit the view was beautiful. It was the first I'd seen it since August of '59.

"Now you got to hold on tight, Cogbill, there might be frozen cowpies under there, and we won't know 'less we hit one and catch a little air."

The hill dropped off steeply for the first fifteen or twenty yards, then adjusted suddenly to a much shallower angle for the remaining hundred-and-fifty or so. This had the effect of giving us a good burst of speed right out of the gate, building up enough momentum to carry us all the way down to the pasture below, over shallow, undulating rolls of earth before petering out in open field. When I looked back, the house was invisible, the ridge of the hilltop breaking line-of-sight.

The first run made the track, packed it down; and in order to preserve it we climbed back up the hill on the north side, heading for the tree at the corner. The second run was better than the first. The snow blew up across the prow of the sled, making us close our eyes, but the track, having been cleared, moved faster and carried us farther across the field at the base of the hill, where we did collide with something and pop up off the ground a good six inches at the end of our run.

The cold turned Ethel's cheeks to apples, and highlighted the freckles on her nose, and in her laughter and her screams of delight as we rode over and over down the hill, I could picture her with her cousins coming here as children. I couldn't help but think what the joyful screams of our own children might sound like echoing across these fields on a day like this one, and with a clarity like the sky, I understood at last the nature of the gift we had been given.

Exhausted, sweating under our heavy coats, we returned Hud's toboggan to his porch, thanked him, and enjoyed a last cup of coffee in his kitchen. Then we got in Ethel's truck and turned North on Owens Drive toward Hooes, which is pronounced "hose," and the humble home of Iris and Elijah Taylor.

Icicles were forming under the eaves of the crooked little house, the dripping water perforating the snow along the front. The tin roof had mostly cleared itself of snow, and the smoke swirled out of the chimney like the souls of the departed.

"You sure this is what you want, Hieronymus?"

"As long as it's okay with you."

"Cogbill, I wouldn't have it any other way."

We sat on the couch in the Taylor's modest living room, under the photos of their seven grown children, Rollie in his Army pink-and-greens, looking ready to liberate all of Europe on his own.

"'Ronymus, what in the hell you doin' out in this stank-ass weather?"

Elijah was in his chair, drinking beer-on-ice in spite of the cold. Iris had her own chair nearby. Ethel helped her with the coffee and then rejoined me on the sofa as Iris took her chair, doilies pinned to the arms and backrest.

"Mr. and Mrs. Taylor," Ethel began. "Hieronymus and I have some news, and then a question we'd like to ask you."

"I sure do hope it ain't nothing bad," Iris said.

"We're expecting."

"Oh! I'm so happy for you."

"My man!"

I took a deep breath. It was my turn. As I looked at them, my eyes welled up in spite of me. I had cut ties with my own family. I had nobody but Ethel. And I understood now that sometimes I would need someone older and wiser, whose experience I could draw upon when my own good sense failed me.

"I don't know how to ask this. I need someone to guide me when I lose my way. I can't replace what I took from you. But I want you to know I love you both."

"Mr. Harry..." Iris had never quite learned to drop the Mr.

I got off the sofa and dropped to my knees, for some reason my eyes were moist and it was difficult to see.

"Mr. Harry. Hieronymus."

Iris got up and put her arms around me. The pain poured out of me like the head on a beer running over the rim, like boiling water lifting the lid off a pot of spaghetti. What the hell, it was only sixteen years late.

"I took your son from you. It was my fault. He was the bravest man I ever knew. He was better than me. I'm so sorry Mom, Pops..."

Eli reached out one brown hand, knobby and twisted with veins, the fingertips flattened and squared from a lifetime of hard labor, and placed it gently on my head.

It was a long moment before I could speak.

"Ethel and I...we want...that is...we'd like to ask you to be our child's godparents."

Now Elijah was a hard man, quick-witted and temperamental, but he was also one of the most honorable men I ever knew. He could fix you with a stare that would put the fear of God in even the most ardent of sinners, and could just as effortlessly make you laugh until you couldn't breathe. But that afternoon as I looked up at him, his face was unreadable. The only sound was Iris's voice.

"Taylor?"

His mouth was a straight line, his nostrils flaring as he breathed. Then I caught a glimmering of moisture at the corner of his eye, and he nodded.

"I guess that be alright."

We drove home in the gathering darkness, the world around us blue with moonlit snow, the twisted black trunks of sleeping trees tangled like a mane on the humped back of the world. Along 301 we passed the Hillcrest Motel and intermittently, modest homes shuttered up against the frigid night. Lights were strung through hedges or around cedars in yards, wreaths hung on doors, the twinkling of Christmas trees through blinds or sheers, and I noted a trace of my mother's perfume and my father's pipe tobacco on the air.

The smell was a sense memory, the kind that accompanies a feeling of a specific time or place. It was the smell of Christmas 1930 in Chesterfield Courthouse, thirty years and a lifetime ago, and I understood that through our child I would see these memories from the other side. We made a right turn where once was the traffic circle at Edge Hill, took Ridge Road to Purkins Corner, then followed Route 3 through King George Courthouse, where decorations had been hung on utility poles and the tree was lit in front of the courthouse. The warmth of hearth and family shone from the homes of Hudson, and Morris; Morgan, Clare, and Clift. Holiday cheer hung over the doors of Trinity Methodist and St. John's Episcopal.

"It's a pretty little town, ain't it, Cogbill?"

I gazed upon the sequined expanse of God's creation, and knew in that moment that there could be no finer town in any world, for here in lowly King George were the people I loved, and nothing else in the infinite, expanding universe could be worth so much. Here, at last, was my home.

"It's wonderful, Ethel."

Late one night the following summer, in a room at Mary Washington Hospital the color of crème-de-menthe, we welcomed Roland William Cogbill into our world, and incredibly, unexpectedly, I found that my life, and all the things I held dear, did not get smaller.

They got larger.